THE HANDSOME MONK
AND OTHER STORIES

WEATHERHEAD BOOKS ON ASIA

THE HANDSOME MONK AND OTHER STORIES

TSERING DÖNDRUP

Translated by Christopher Peacock

COLUMBIA UNIVERSITY PRESS
New York

Columbia University Press wishes to express its appreciation for
assistance given by the Pushkin Fund in the publication of this book.

This publication has been supported by the Richard W. Weatherhead Publication
Fund of the Weatherhead East Asian Institute, Columbia University.

Columbia University Press
Publishers Since 1893
New York   Chichester, West Sussex
cup.columbia.edu

Library of Congress Cataloging-in-Publication Data
Names: Tshe-ring-don-grub, 1961– author. | Peacock, Christopher, 1986– translator.
Title: The handsome monk and other stories / Tsering Dondrup ;
translated by Christopher Peacock.
Description: New York : Columbia University Press, 2019. |
Series: Weatherhead books on Asia | Includes bibliographical references.
Identifiers: LCCN 2018020462 (print) | LCCN 2018027037 (ebook) |
ISBN 9780231548786 (electronic) | ISBN 9780231190220 (cloth : alk. paper) |
ISBN 9780231190237 (pbk.)
Classification: LCC PL3748.T776 (ebook) | LCC PL3748.T776 A2 2019 (print) |
DDC 895/.43—dc23
LC record available at https://lccn.loc.gov/2018020462

Columbia University Press books are printed on permanent and
durable acid-free paper.
Printed in the United States of America
Cover design: Noah Arlow

CONTENTS

THE HANDSOME MONK
AND OTHER STORIES

Introduction

CORRUPT LAMAS, RELIABLE YAKS: THE FICTIONAL WORLD OF TSERING DÖNDRUP

"A monk and a prostitute. Aren't we the perfect match?" So says the protagonist of "The Handsome Monk" when he finds himself entangled in a relationship hardly appropriate for a man of his occupation. For the wayward monk the match may not be ideal, but as a juxtaposition that captures the unique fictional world contained in these pages, it couldn't be more fitting. This is Tibet, where to this day monastic life remains commonplace and some form of religious devotion is the norm for most. But Tibet is also a place in the real world, where real problems exist and human motivations and failings are as applicable as anywhere else. The stories in this volume bring to life modern Tibet as imagined by the perceptive, critical, and humorous author Tsering Döndrup, a writer who has been a fixture on the Tibetan literary scene since his debut in the 1980s. His is a world where lamas drive expensive cars, where nomads consider committing murder to escape gambling debts, where corruption is rife and happy resolutions are hard to come by. Shangri-La it is not.

Tsering Döndrup's first story appeared in 1983, and to date he has published two collections of short stories, a collection of novellas, and four full-length novels. He was born in 1961 in Malho

(Ch.: Henan) Mongolian Autonomous County in Qinghai province, China. To Tibetans, this broader region is known as Amdo, the easternmost part of the Tibetan-inhabited areas, which now spreads largely across China's northwest provinces of Qinghai and Gansu. As a child, Tsering Döndrup helped his family tend their livestock and didn't begin attending school until the age of thirteen. In 1982 he graduated from the Huangnan Teacher's Training School, and he continued his studies at the Qinghai Nationalities Institute in Xining and the Northwest Nationalities Institute in Lanzhou (both since renamed as "universities"), two of the most prestigious institutions for the study of Tibetan culture. It is virtually impossible for modern Tibetan writers to live off the income from their art alone, and Tsering Döndrup is no exception: he has worked as a schoolteacher, a legal secretary, and an editor at the office of the Henan County Annals. In 2013, however, he retired to focus on his writing full-time, a promising indication that his career shows no signs of slowing down.

While he is widely considered to be a Tibetan author, Tsering Döndrup is, by ethnicity, Mongolian. The author's home county of Malho (also referred to by Tibetans as *sogpo*, the Tibetan word for "Mongolian") is a historically Mongolian county in a Tibetan region whose inhabitants trace their heritage to the arrival of Gushri Khan in the seventeenth century. Over time, however, its people gradually assimilated into Tibetan culture and adopted the Tibetan language, and today the people of Malho occupy something of an in-between space: ethnically Mongolian, culturally and linguistically Tibetan.[1] Though this intermediate status has reportedly led some to question the extent of Tsering Döndrup's "Tibetanness," the vast majority of Tibetan readers have embraced

---

1. Yangdon Dhondup, "Writers at the Crossroads: The Mongolian-Tibetan Authors Tsering Dondup and Jangbu," *Inner Asia* 4, no. 2 (2002): 225–240.

him as their own, and his reputation as one of modern Tibet's most talented, popular, and critically acclaimed authors is beyond question.

His identity as a Tibetan writer is reflected in his deep engagement with the long and rich traditions of Tibetan literature, which stretch all the way back to the *glu* and *mgur* poem-songs found in the caves of Dunhuang. Much premodern Tibetan writing relates in one form or another to the subject of Buddhism, and it comes in all shapes and sizes. In terms of poetry (and Tibetan *belles lettres* in general), one text above all looms large, and that is Daṇḍin's *Kāvyādarśa* (*The Mirror of Poetry*). Translated into Tibetan from Sanskrit in the thirteenth century, Daṇḍin's text had an impact that is hard to overstate, setting poetic guidelines for everything from metrics to specific synonyms. Narrative prose also existed (though more often than not it was interspersed with verse of various kinds, making many premodern Tibetan texts rather stylistically eclectic), particularly in the numerous examples of biography and autobiography.[2] Lastly, there is the broad category of folk and oral literature, included in which is the *Epic of King Gesar*, sometimes said to be the longest epic in the world.

In the present collection, one need only read "A Show to Delight the Masses" to see how Tsering Döndrup has inherited key aspects of this legacy. The story borrows the traditional narrative form of mixed prose and poetry and updates it in a distinctly

---

2. For more on Tibet's various traditional poetic forms and the influence of *The Mirror of Poetry*, see Roger R. Jackson, "'Poetry' in Tibet: *Glu, mGur, sNyan ngag* and 'Songs of Experience'," and Leonard W. J. van der Kuijp, "Tibetan Belles-Lettres: The Influence of Daṇḍin and Kṣemendra," in *Tibetan Literature: Studies in Genre*, ed. José Ignacio Cabezón and Roger R. Jackson (Ithaca, NY: Snow Lion, 1996), 368–392 and 393–410. Janet Gyatso's *Apparitions of the Self: The Secret Autobiographies of a Tibetan Visionary* (Princeton, NJ: Princeton University Press, 1998) provides an excellent introduction to Tibetan biographical writing.

playful, modern fashion, and its subject matter references at least two kinds of traditional texts. It is a close relative of the genre of *delok* tales, which narrate the experiences of ordinary people who, like the story's protagonist, Lozang Gyatso, take a brief trip to Hell and back (in Lozang Gyatso's case, however, that return is short-lived).[3] The story also recalls a famous episode from *The Epic of King Gesar* in which the king travels to Hell to rescue his wife, who has been put on trial before the Lord of Death.

But it will be immediately clear to the reader that these are no traditional Tibetan texts. They are composed as modern short stories, and in that sense are perfectly legible to a contemporary global audience. At times, Tsering Döndrup even plays with narrative style in a way that pushes his work into the territory of avant-garde experimentation: "A Formula," for example, leaps through time in a manner disorienting for reader and protagonist alike. A recent study has cautioned us not to see a gulf between Tibet's rich writing traditions and its modern literature, and there is certainly a case to be made for continuity, be it in terms of *kāvya* poetics or the influence of oral storytelling on modern narrative.[4] But for all the ways the Tibetan literature we now call modern may be building on its past, there are countless more ways it is forging ahead to create new and unexplored possibilities. The introduction of short stories and novels, never before recognized forms in Tibetan literature, is but one example of these revolutionary developments (the eighteenth-century *Tale of the Incomparable Prince*, a Buddhist-themed retelling of the *Ramayana*, is somewhat exceptional for having an overtly fictional plot, but it possesses all the traits of an epic and none of the modern novel).

---

3. Bryan Cuevas has examined this genre in detail in *Travels in the Netherworld: Buddhist Popular Narratives of Death and the Afterlife in Tibet* (Oxford: Oxford University Press, 2008).

4. Lama Jabb, *Oral and Literary Continuities in Modern Tibetan Literature: The Inescapable Nation* (Lanham, MD: Lexington Books, 2015).

Modern Tibetan literature has also undergone a transformation in content. There are still stories or poems about religion—Buddhism remains an integral part of Tibetan life—but they are likely to be about the practice or the effects of religion in the everyday world; no longer is this literature that we would call explicitly "religious." Moreover, this everyday life is that of Tibetans in modern China, which brings us to an entirely different literary landscape that Tsering Döndrup also inhabits.

The very fact of Tibet's inclusion in the People's Republic of China (PRC) has necessarily produced an enormous shift in its literature, as writing that reflects the experiences of modern Tibetans must now reflect a life colored and conditioned by the experience of existing in contemporary China. In addition, Tibetans now find themselves labeled a "minority nationality"—along with China's fifty-four officially designated others—and their literature therefore also labeled a "minority literature." In terms of production, Tibetan creative writing is entirely integrated into China's state and private literary systems. Tibetan authors publish through journals and publishers organized under Chinese state practices, and likewise, online literature is largely circulated on websites and platforms hosted in China. Unlike the multifaceted heritage of *belles lettres* described previously, these developments are all recent. It was, by and large, in the political thaw that followed the Cultural Revolution (1966–1976) that this new kind of literature began to emerge. Two journals in particular, *Tibetan Art and Literature*, launched in Lhasa in 1980, and *Light Rain*, launched in Xining in 1981, helped to foment a virtual explosion of new Tibetan writing (many of Tsering Döndrup's stories have been published in both over the years).

In 1983, the latter journal published a free-verse poem, often said to be the first of its kind in Tibetan, called "Waterfall of Youth." This freewheeling, impassioned call for a progressive renewal of Tibetan culture to be led by a new generation was a revelation for Tibetan readers. Its author, Döndrup Gyel, has since been enshrined as the "father" of modern Tibetan literature.[5] Though his career was short (Döndrup Gyel committed suicide in 1985), his influence can hardly be exaggerated. His work is still read today at poetry recitations held in his honor; a growing body of "Döndrup Gyel research" examines his work from all angles; and his six-volume collected works is a constant presence in Tibetan bookshops. While Döndrup Gyel's legacy remains a dominant force in Tibetan literature, a number of talented authors with diverse styles have emerged in the years since his time, and along with them numerous other journals of fiction, poetry, and essayistic writing. There is now a robust publishing industry and a market for novels and book-length collections of poetry and short stories, and in recent years online literary journals and self-publishing through new media have soared in popularity. In the West, a gradual response to this new literary activity has occurred in the form of academic studies and translations that, though few, are increasing in number.[6]

One more of Tsering Döndrup's literary circles deserves mention: that of world literature. Like many modern Tibetan writers, Tsering Döndrup has encountered foreign literature primarily through Chinese translations. While he admires select modern Chinese authors (Lu Xun, for example), Tsering Döndrup is most of all interested in global literary currents beyond China's borders. He counts George Orwell as one of his favorite

---

5. There are numerous studies of Döndrup Gyel's work in the Tibetan language, and several articles in English. For an overview of the author and this poem in particular, see Lauran R. Hartley, "The Advent of Modern Tibetan Free-Verse Poetry in the Tibetan Language," in *A New Literary History of Modern China*, ed. David Der-wei Wang (Cambridge, MA: Belknap Press, 2017), 765–771.

6. The most significant publication in English remains *Modern Tibetan Literature and Social Change* (Durham, NC: Duke University Press, 2008), edited by Lauran R. Hartley and Patricia Schiaffini-Vedani.

writers and is particularly fond of a number of nineteenth-century Russian authors: Nikolai Gogol, Ivan Goncharov, and Mikhail Lermontov, among others. While foreign literature in translation has been influencing Tibetan writers in new and unexpected ways, Tsering Döndrup's work itself has begun to enter into global conversations, having already been translated into English, French, German, Chinese, Mongolian, Japanese, and other languages. Through these multidirectional engagements, his writing is beginning to find the audiences it merits and helping to create a space for modern Tibetan literature on a global stage from which it has too long been absent.

English-language readers experiencing Tsering Döndrup's stories for the first time will discover a vivid fictional world that repeatedly returns to the same settings, the same themes, the same issues, and sometimes even the same characters. Almost all of the stories take place in the fictional county of Tsezhung, a rural nomad locale that lies along the real-life Tsechu River in his home region of Malho, Qinghai. The author's creation of a consistent setting for his fictional world immediately calls to mind illustrious counterparts such as Faulkner's Yoknapatawpha County or, slightly closer to home, Mo Yan's Northeast Gaomi Township, but the reader will never have encountered a setting quite like Tsezhung, a quintessential Tibetan nomadic landscape where small communities of herders shepherd their flocks across vast, open grasslands thousands of feet above sea level. The characters subsist on a diet of staple nomad fare—meat, butter, cheese, *tsampa* (a doughlike ball of roasted barely flour mixed with other ingredients)—and go about their daily business to the ever-present rhythms of Tibetan religious life.

But the briefest dip into "Brothers" or "Revenge," both of which portray violent feuds between nomad clans, will be enough to show that Tsering Döndrup hardly presents an idealized or idyllic picture of this striking setting. Tsering Döndrup's fiction is unflaggingly critical, reflective, and above all, satirical. There is also a practical reason for his invention of a fictional county: to insulate himself against the potential for readers to see in his stories reflections of real-life events or people, not entirely unlikely given that the author has lived his entire life in a relatively close-knit community. For example, Alak Drong is a recurring character whose unscrupulous ways will quickly become all too familiar to the reader. In the Amdo dialect of Tibetan, "Alak" is the equivalent of "Rinpoché," a term used in Central Tibet and in exile as a respectful form of address for a senior religious teacher. This could be a lama (a term for various types of Buddhist teacher) or a *trülku* (a reincarnated lama). "Drong" is the Tibetan word for a wild yak, a particularly fierce and untamable ancestor of Tibet's emblematic animal. This is a comically improbable name for a revered master of the Buddha Dharma, and it was a very conscious choice on Tsering Döndrup's part, as any name that inadvertently resembled that of an actual lama or *trülku* could have brought down unwanted troubles on the author's head.

Alak Drong is the foremost symbol of Tsering Döndrup's wide-ranging and unflinching critique of corruption and hypocrisy in the modern-day practice of Tibetan Buddhism. This comes in the form of an excessive alms-giving campaign that reduces an already impoverished community to virtual destitution in "The Disturbance in D— Camp," the protagonist's various naïve misadventures in "Ralo," and the profane hypocrisies of Gendün Gyatso in "The Handsome Monk." But we must also be cautious not to read his work oversimplistically as being somehow "antireligious." The last story is a case in point. Like the best of authors, Tsering Döndrup is not didactic but explorative and, while critical, empathetic. "The Handsome Monk" does not condemn its protagonist; rather, it paints a brutally honest picture of the psychological traumas and dilemmas faced by a man who, while he may be a monk, is also a person, complete with the flaws, desires, and contradictions of all human beings. We might even say that "The Handsome Monk" could be read as a deft fictional rendering of Buddhist philosophical concerns about the insignificance of the mundane world, not unlike a tale about the worldly temptations of a Catholic priest. In general, readers looking for modern-day reflections of Tibetan Buddhist practice in these pages will find them in abundance. "Revenge," for instance, is an exploration of karmic cause and effect executed with a conciseness and poignancy that is particular to the short story form. Unlike the great corpus of Tibetan literature that precedes his work, however, Tsering Döndrup's fiction does not advocate any particular solution to the problems he poses; we are not told that the cycle of samsaric suffering can only end through Buddhist practice leading to liberation. Perhaps the answer does lie in the cultivation of compassion and merit, or in very real-world laws and policies, or both: his stories, tantalizingly ambiguous, give readers room to consider these problems for themselves.

Religious figures are by no means the only target of the author's satire. Again and again we witness the corruption of insatiable officials in a socialist system whose raison d'être is supposedly to "serve the people"—the very people they end up exploiting. These are officials of the Chinese government bureaucracy, but more often than not they are corrupt and callous Tibetan cadres, such as the farcically devious Lozang Gyatso in "A Show to Delight the Masses," the red-haired woman in "Black Fox Valley," and the unnamed narrator of "Notes of a Volunteer AIDS Worker." In fact, virtually no one emerges unscathed from the author's barbed pen, bar the ever-reliable yak. In "Ralo," we are even treated to a skewering of naïve Western tourists with their romantic preconceptions of an untainted Tibetan "pure land." Beyond his critiques of individual and institutional failings, Tsering Döndrup is often at his best when examining the social consequences that China's unchecked drive to modernization has brought to the Tibetan highlands: gambling, prostitution, and alcoholism are just some of the social ills in "Mahjong," "Nose Rings," "The Handsome Monk," and "Notes of a Volunteer AIDS Worker" (gambling also brings with it a dimension of ethnic politics, as it most often comes in the form of an addiction to the Chinese game of mahjong). But no matter what the context, Tsering Döndrup is above all concerned with the hardships faced by ordinary Tibetans in a world that is both rapidly changing and yet somehow immutable. With knowledge acquired through a lifetime of firsthand experience, he presents his nomad characters in countless guises: hardworking, lazy, clever, gullible, strong, vulnerable—but never idealized and never demonized.

The setting for Tsering Döndrup's fiction also plays a role that goes beyond mere backdrop. The author has exhibited a consistent concern with environmental issues, and in the case of Tibet— home to numerous endangered species and a vast repository of fresh water resources (many of Asia's largest rivers originate on the Tibetan plateau)—these are problems with global repercussions. In recent decades Tibetan Buddhism has become closely aligned in many quarters with environmental awareness and activism, but Tsering Döndrup's approach to the question as a writer is perhaps more resonant with the global environmental justice movement, particularly in his concern for the traditional relationship between people and land (in that sense, not unlike the way many Native American groups have been prominent in environmental justice efforts in the United States).

In Tsering Döndrup's fiction, the degradation of Tibet's environment goes hand in hand with the decline of traditional nomad life brought about by industrialization and China's rapid charge to modernity. "The Story of the Moon," a dystopian sci-fi vignette, casts a pessimistic eye over the consequences of humanity embracing reckless technological development as its guiding ethos. "Black

Fox Valley," meanwhile, shows this process on a much more human scale. The story opens with a description of the Edenic valley, filled with an abundance of natural riches that even "an expert in botany would be hard pressed to identify." When Sangyé's family leaves Black Fox Valley, they become mired in the realities of modern industrial and consumer life, every example of which turns out to be a pale and impractical imitation of their tried-and-tested traditional ways. Finally, they give up on this new world and return home only to discover, in a tragic inversion of the story's introduction, that the idyllic valley has been turned into one giant coal mine (rampant strip mining is one of the gravest threats to Tibet's pastoral lands). Tsering Döndrup's story illustrates that Tibetan nomads, who have lived in harmony with their environment for centuries, have a lot more to tell us about modernity than we might think.

Of the stories collected here, "Ralo" also deserves particular mention, as it is one of the most well-known works of fiction in the burgeoning canon of modern Tibetan literature. Just as the introduction to the second part of the story says, it was first published in *Light Rain* magazine in 1991, and a longer "sequel" arrived in 1997, thus turning it into a novella. The anecdote related by the narrator at the start of part 2 is true: the editorial department of *Light Rain* really did request that Tsering Döndrup concoct an optimistic conclusion to his story and turn Ralo into a successful and inspirational character. The self-reflective anxiety that Ralo prompted among Tibetan readers was by no means limited to these literary editors. In a landmark article first published in 2001, the noted critic Dülha Gyel set out a detailed analysis of Ralo, concluding that he represents no less than a crystallization of all the ills of the Tibetan character. Foremost among Ralo's faults, he argued, are his particularly "Tibetan" reliance on superstition and faith to guide him through life and his absorption of a Buddhist conviction in the absence of the self, making Ralo lazy and incapable of applying himself to progress in the real world. To readers of Chinese literature this will sound familiar, and for good reason, as Dülha Gyel's analysis consciously built on the discourse of national character that was so prominent at the birth of modern Chinese writing. "The True Story of Ah Q," by modern China's most renowned author, Lu Xun, caused countless readers, writers, and scholars to plunge into considerations of what was wrong with the Chinese "national character," with many people even fretting that the story's titular character somehow reflected or represented them. In the years since the publication of "Ralo," a number of articles about the story have been published and have gradually coalesced into a similar debate about Ralo's personality flaws and the deep-seated cultural factors that may lie behind them.

Quite what the reader unfamiliar with or indifferent to such a reading will make of the story is another matter. While Tsering Döndrup is a great admirer of Lu Xun's work, he remains ambivalent about the comparisons elicited by his story. And indeed, "Ralo" is teasing, ambiguous, and hard to pin a single reading upon. Ralo may be lazy and foolish, but he is also talented (initially, at least) at a number of endeavors. He may be gullible and absurd, but he is also the victim of social forces far beyond his control. However we might read "Ralo," it is not a stretch to say that it has had an influence on modern Tibetan literature that is almost comparable to Ah Q's influence on its Chinese counterpart. Ralo's presence even extends beyond the literary realm: there are cafés scattered throughout China's Tibetan regions named after the (in)famous character where one can order a "Ralo milk tea."

The issues faced by nomads (and indeed all Tibetans) in modern China are also embedded in the very language of these stories. The Chinese language has had a huge impact on modern Tibetan, from numerous loanwords that have slipped into everyday speech to the many political and administrative terms phonetically borrowed from Mandarin. Tsering Döndrup treats this linguistic crisis quite unlike any other contemporary Tibetan author. "Piss and Pride" sketches the social and linguistic misadventures of one elderly nomad who must take a trip to the city to see his son (along the way providing a wry send-up of the discourse of "national pride," ubiquitous in Tibetan intellectual circles since the time of Döndrup Gyel), but it is in "Black Fox Valley" that the linguistic crisis of modern Tibetan is dealt with most poignantly.

As his career has progressed, Tsering Döndrup has continued to refine his style while pushing new boundaries, and "Black Fox Valley" is the most outstanding example of his more recent work. The immediate context for the piece is a government campaign to "Return the Pastures and Restore the Grasslands," part of the broader "Open up the West" campaign launched in 1999 to promote economic development in China's western regions, some of the poorest in the country. As part of the plan to "retire" grazing pastures, large numbers of nomad communities have been taken off the land they traditionally used and resettled in newly constructed towns.[7] In "Black Fox Valley," we see what happens to one family that undergoes this relocation. As shown in the story, the monumental shift in lifestyle has had dire consequences for many. In addition to the problems caused by shoddy housing construction, many resettled nomads have had to wrestle with alcoholism, gambling, and prostitution—all perennial concerns of Tsering Döndrup's penetrating stories about Tibetan society.

But the story is much more than a mere critique of a specific government policy. Tibetan nomadic life is the heartbeat of

7. For more on these campaigns, see Emily T. Yeh, "Green Governmentality and Pastoralism in Western China: 'Converting Pastures to Grasslands'," *Nomadic Peoples* 9, no. 1/2 (2005): 9–30.

Tsering Döndrup's fiction, and "Black Fox Valley" charts not only the forced decline of an entire way of existence that has persisted uninterrupted for centuries but also the cultural and linguistic alienation inherent in this process. Through its liberal use of Chinese vocabulary (rendered phonetically in Tibetan in the original), the story shows that the nomads must not only confront unfamiliar settings but also experience them through an unfamiliar language. In his native environment, the father, Sangyé, is a respected member of the community, quick-witted and adept at verbal sparring. After their move to the town, however, his inability to speak Chinese and his inexperience with settled, "modern" life quickly turn him into a figure of ridicule, an ignorant bumpkin scorned by the Chinese-speaking local official. We see also just how quickly nomad life can be erased through the family's generational differences: while Jamyang, the grandfather, is incapable of adapting to this new lifestyle, the granddaughter, Lhari Kyi, adjusts quite happily, nowhere more so than in her speech, which becomes peppered with Chinese phrases. In a sense, "Black Fox Valley" represents a microcosm of Tsering Döndrup's most closely held literary concerns, crystallized into a virtuosic and deeply empathetic narrative: the corruption of both religion and officialdom, the degradation of traditional nomad life and its attendant social issues, the linguistic invasion of the Chinese language, and the threat to Tibet's environment from industrial modernity.

These stories will provide a fresh experience for readers of every stripe. For those interested in Tibetan culture, there is a keen inquiry into how it persists in a modernizing world that threatens its very existence. For those interested in contemporary China, there is a depiction of its ethnic and linguistic politics that brings to light a greatly overlooked dimension of the PRC. And for readers seeking new perspectives in contemporary fiction, they are here in abundance. Modern Tibetan literature may still be an unknown quantity to English-speaking audiences, but for an introduction to its vibrancy and vitality, we could ask for no better guide than Tsering Döndrup.

A NOTE ON ROMANIZATION

Tibetan personal and place names, as well as other instances of Tibetan vocabulary in the text, are rendered, with minor deviations, using David Germano and Nicolas Tournadre's "Simplified Phonetic Transcription of Standard Tibetan," developed by the Tibetan and Himalayan Library. Chinese terms are rendered according to the Hanyu Pinyin romanization system.

ACKNOWLEDGMENTS

All translations in this volume are my own, with the exception of "A Show to Delight the Masses," which was translated by Lauran Hartley and appeared previously in *Persimmon* magazine. I would like to thank Lauran not only for allowing me to include her excellent translation but also for her unfailingly selfless assistance with the project as a whole. Part 1 of "Ralo" was previously published in *Old Demons, New Deities* (OR Books, 2017), and benefited from the editorial suggestions of Tenzin Dickie. I would like to thank Christine Dunbar at Columbia University Press for providing expert guidance throughout the publishing process, as well as Chloe Estep and Max Berwald, who gave invaluable suggestions on the translations. Several Tibetan friends helped me with linguistic queries, in particular Tsering Samdrup, who was extremely generous with his time and his wealth of knowledge. None of this would have been possible without the loving and unwavering support of my wife, Jennie Chow, who has been my constant companion in several homes around the world and has always been my first and most dedicated reader as well as a wonderfully perceptive editor. Lastly, I owe a great debt of gratitude to the author. From the very beginning he has encouraged and assisted this project in every way he can, not least by patiently responding to my interminable questions. I hope this book can go some way toward helping earn his work the wider audience it so richly deserves.

1

THE DISTURBANCE IN D— CAMP

ONE

Something like this really did happen. As soon as it took place I wrote a report and sent it to the county government, who, after marking it with the words "situation verified" and affixing an official seal, sent it on to some Tibetan newspaper. About a year passed, and there was still no response. Later, I found out from a friend of mine that the editor of the paper had buried my report in a corner of the office, muttering, "We've been hearing a lot about this sort of thing lately; got to be careful, have to be careful." For this reason I decided to change the names of the people and places involved and write it up as a story.

TWO

Sökyab, the head of D— Camp, was up early. Riding a black yak, he passed by every family's door. "Soon as you've put the cattle out, the head of each family get to my place for a meeting!" he called out as he went. The yak's lips had turned completely white from the frost, and it was panting heavily. From a distance, it looked like two columns of white smoke were spouting from its nostrils.

Sökyab took a silver-plated snuffbox from the pocket of his *chuba*, tipped a little bit onto the nail of his left thumb, and snorted it up into two nostrils that were so small it was hard to tell whether or not they existed. Wiping his thumb on the inside of his *chuba*, he took a look around. "Right, everyone's here, we can make a start. I'll keep it brief today. It won't be long until the monastery puts up the pillar in the assembly hall. Our camp needs to contribute one hundred yuan per person to begin with, and if you've no money you can give a good-quality ram." He put the snuffbox away and retrieved a greasy notebook from his *chuba*. "In my family, for example, there are five people, so that would be five hundred yuan, or if it was rams, five rams. In Akhu Tamdrin's family there are eight people. If he gives cash then it's eight hundred yuan, if he gives rams then it's eight rams. In Akhu Zöpa's family there are eleven people. If he gives cash then it's one thousand one hundred yuan, if he gives rams then it's eleven rams . . ."

The attendees of the meeting, eyes wide and mouths agape, began to whisper among themselves. Sökyab snapped his notebook shut and raised his voice. "You all know how many people are in each of your families, so I don't need to list them all individually. You ought to know that the building of the assembly hall is for the benefit of all sentient beings, and it's for your own benefit too. Whoever fails to contribute will be kicked out of the camp. No one in the camp will be allowed to speak to that family, and they won't be allowed to pitch their tents with us, either. Oh, and one more thing: counting from today, all the money needs to be handed over within a month."

Everyone was left even more wide-eyed and agape than before. Thus concluded the meeting, the first of its kind since the founding of New China.

THREE

The men of D— Camp had been gathering money for about twenty days. Most of the families had counted up the cash according to the family head count and handed it over to Sökyab, but Akhu Zöpa's family had only managed to save up two hundred and thirty yuan.

"We still need eight hundred and seventy yuan," he sighed. "Where on earth are we going to get it?" Old Zöpa was so worried that he even lost his appetite. In the past, his family had been one of the more prosperous in the camp, but recently they'd taken two trips to Lhasa, and, more seriously, the previous summer their flock of sheep had been carried away by a flood. Since then they'd fallen into destitution.

There was also Ama Drölkar and her daughter, who every year relied on the government to get them through the hard times. Normally they couldn't even afford to buy tea and salt, so how were they going to scrape up a two hundred-yuan donation?

Every day Sökyab did a circuit around the camp, yelling, "Time to pay up!"

When a month had passed, Sökyab got all the family heads together and convened another meeting. He took a good pinch of snuff before beginning. "Right, most of the families with cash have now handed over the cash, and those without have handed over the rams. Yes indeed, very good. If you're a black-headed Tibetan then that's what you ought to do. However—," and here, he raised his voice, "Yes, *some* families—have not paid up. Yes indeed, very good. Haha! And where will those people end up when they die? Have a think about that. I'll keep it brief today. What we talked about before—I'm sure you all remember. When we move to the spring camp, those two families will be out on their own."

Ama Drölkar wasn't at the meeting. Akhu Zöpa headed home, muttering to himself. "My god, even back in the Old Society and in the Cultural Revolution an old man like me was never expelled from the camp! Snub-nosed Sökyab, death's too good for you! Not even a dog would eat that corpse. You . . .!" He was shaking so badly that he fell of the back of his yak and died.

FOUR

Sökyab took the cash from D— Camp and herded the donated rams to the monastery.

"*Ah la la!*" he announced upon his arrival. "The Dharma protectors look so alive! Old man Zöpa didn't give any money for the building of the assembly hall, so he fell off his yak and died."

"Well of course he did, of course he did," said the monks. From then on, they would mention this to anyone they met: "Did you hear about what happened to old Zöpa?"

Alak Drong, the head of the monastery, praised Sökyab profusely for bringing in the donations by the deadline he had set. "How much can your camp put up for the building of the stupa?" the lama asked Sökyab.

"How much did the other camps say they'd give?"

"The lowest was thirty a head, the highest fifty a head."

"Then I'll commit to sixty," said Sökyab without the slightest hesitation, and headed back to the camp to convene another meeting.

"Alak Drong has conferred great praise on our camp! Hmmm— yes." Sökyab snorted a generous helping of snuff into his right nostril before continuing. "This spring they're building a stupa. Hmmm—yes." He snorted a smaller amount of snuff into his left nostril, and wiped his thumb on the inside of his *chuba*. He took out the notebook, so sticky with filth it looked like a used handkerchief, and opened it up. "So it's sixty per person. In my family there are five people, five sixes is thirty, so that's three hundred yuan . . ."

Seeing that everyone was whispering among themselves, he snapped the notebook shut and paused for a moment. "You all know how many people are in each of your families. Whoever doesn't pay up by the time we move to the summer camp—well, getting kicked out of the camp is nothing. If you get on the wrong side of the Dharma protectors, then . . . I'm sure you all get the idea." And with that the meeting was adjourned.

FIVE

One morning shortly after they had moved to the spring camp, Sökyab was riding his yak around and shouting like a man possessed. "Time to pay up! If you don't pay up, you'll be kicked out of the camp! If you don't pay up you'll be out there with them!" Spurring on his yak, he pointed toward the solitary tents of the Zöpa family (now named the Yarpel family, after the eldest son) and the Drölkar family. "If you don't pay up then you'll be out there with them!" Though he made eight or so rounds of the camp, only seven families emerged to offer their donations. Sökyab was enraged. "Enemies of the Dharma!" he screamed. "You're all out of the camp!" And so the majority of the families were sent off in the direction of the Yarpel and Drölkar families.

Sökyab presented his roughly five thousand yuan to Alak Drong. "What the hell is this? That's it?" he demanded, staring at Sökyab in disbelief.

"Most of the families didn't give anything." Sökyab heaved a sigh. "Of course you know how much I urged them."

Alak Drong too heaved a sigh. "Yes indeed, the people of this degenerate era really are stingy. No piety at all. Noble Avalokiteśvara, how pitiful are the people of this degenerate era! So how much money can your camp put up for the assembly hall?"

"How much did the other camps say they'd put up?"

"Not counting the money for the pillars, one or two hundred a head."

Sökyab despaired (his family too was now very low on money). "If I promised a lot now then I'd just be racking up the offenses.

Those enemies of the Dharma won't give a penny. But I can do my best to persuade them!"

"Then you've got to have the money by May."

"Yes, of course."

Returning to the camp, he paid a visit to the few remaining families that hadn't been expelled. He told them about the importance of building the assembly hall, and how if they didn't give a donation then being kicked out of the camp would be the least of their worries, that old man Zöpa is an example of what happens when you get on the wrong side of the Dharma protectors, and plenty more besides. Finally, he laid out his solemn conclusion: "So, this time, if you can't get the money from the earth, get it from the sky. If anyone comes to me saying they haven't got the money, I'll have only one thing to say to them: when we move to the summer pasture, you're out of the camp."

SIX

When D— Camp moved to its summer pasture, it consisted solely of the tent of the Sökyab family; everyone else had been "kicked out of the camp." At first he refused to speak to anyone at all, and they refused to speak to him. There's nothing wrong with one person refusing to speak to everyone else, but everyone else refusing to speak to just one person, well, that's a truly unbearable state of affairs. Sökyab, unable to take it any longer, jumped on his yak and rode around calling out, "Everyone come back to the camp! Everyone come back to the camp!" But no one paid him the least bit of attention.

Sökyab took his complaint to the township government. "I've been kicked out of the camp," he informed them.

"How can a thing like that happen in this day and age? Impossible."

Sökyab took his complaint to the county government. "I've been kicked out of the camp," he informed them.

"Impossible. Seems like there's something wrong with your brain. Get yourself to the hospital."

It seemed like there really was something wrong with his brain. He spent the whole day riding around madly from door to door shouting, "Come back to the camp! Whoever doesn't come back to the camp will be kicked out of the camp!" In the end his yak's tongue was sticking out of its mouth by a whole foot and a mixture of blood and sweat dripped off its back. No matter how much he whipped it, it wouldn't move an inch.

SEVEN

"Everyone come back to the camp!" The next day, and for many days after, Sökyab continued to run about shouting, "Come back to the camp! Whoever doesn't come back to the camp will be kicked out of the camp!"

"Eh, snub-nosed Sökyab really has gone nuts."

"Completely nuts. What a shame."

"A real shame. Even more so for his wife and kids."

"Well, what's past is past," said Yarpel. "As long as you don't object, I think we should do something about it."

"..."

The masses are indeed compassionate. Everyone invited him to come back to the camp, and his family was restored to the community. They sent Sökyab to the hospital to receive psychiatric care, and he is turning back into a normal person. As long as that "old affliction" doesn't flare up again . . .

2

PISS AND PRIDE

It was almost the end of the ninth month in the Tibetan calendar, but it was still hot in the city, on top of which his fur jacket was a bit too thick, making him sweat profusely and feel an unbearable thirst. He really regretted that he hadn't worn something lighter yesterday. When he thought about it, though, there wasn't much he could have done, since when he'd left the house the previous morning it was raining and snowing, and a cold wind was blowing—not exactly "home sweet home." Fortunately, he didn't have to go too far before he came across a place selling tea and other drinks beneath a big multicolored parasol. He drank several cups of tea in succession, then continued to roam the shops looking for the radio his neighbors had asked him to get.

He had no idea how far he'd walked, but when he turned to look he could see the college building where his son went to school—the one decorated with the eight auspicious signs—standing out clearly among the other tall buildings like the moon amid the stars. This gave him some comfort, and he kept going.

After a while he felt the need to take a piss, and he remembered what his son had said to him: "If nature calls, you have to go to the public toilet. There are lots of them on the main roads. If you pee any old place, then getting a fine would be the least of

our worries—you'd be harming the reputation of our nationality."
He looked around, but nowhere was there a building resembling
this "public toilet" he had in mind, so he kept going.

He saw a few men go into a building, then emerge shortly after,
doing up their trousers as they went. Could this be the public
toilet? he wondered. But this building was even nicer than the
dorms at his son's university, and when he approached the doorway he was met by a drifting aroma of incense. *No way*, he thought,
and decided not to go in.

By this point his bladder was on the verge of bursting. He
stopped a passerby and said, "*Arok*, buddy, ah . . ." then made some
gestures with his hands (he wasn't a mute, but he didn't know
Chinese, so what else could he do?). "You're the *aluo*, not me!"
the man replied in Chinese and stormed off.[1]

"Eh, I wish I knew some Chinese," he mumbled to himself. He
scanned the area until his gaze finally fell on the secluded corner
he was after, but immediately he remembered "the reputation of
our nationality" and forced himself to hold it in.

"Best if I just get back quick as possible," he thought, turning
around and picking up his pace. Soon he was half trotting half
running, and then he broke into a full-blown sprint. This was the
first time since he'd turned forty or fifty that he'd run like a kid,
full tilt. Unfortunately, a sudden unbearable pressure doubled him
up, and he was left clutching his crotch as he supported himself
with each heavy step forward.

The building decorated with the eight auspicious signs seemed
so close—how come he still hadn't gotten there yet? Before his
eyes all was grassland, where anywhere you turned there were

---

1. *Arok* (friend, buddy) is a common term of greeting in Tibetan. *Aluo*,
its approximate pronunciation in Chinese, is a derogatory term used by
Han Chinese to refer to Tibetans.

countless places you could piss to your heart's content, completely worry free. Oh what a wonderful thing it is, to take a carefree piss!

The tall buildings in front of him began to wave back and forth.

"Ah, I can't hold it anymore!" He came to a halt, but then he thought of the previous evening when his son's college friends were talking about how every time someone from their hometown came to the city they committed some "faux pas" or other, and he thought about the angry and pained expressions on each of their faces. *I can see why the youngsters get mad. I mustn't bring shame on the next generation*, he thought, and like a wounded man filled with resentment he clenched his jaw, bit his lip, and continued to drive himself onward. Finally, he arrived at the main gate of the college building decorated with the eight auspicious signs. When he regained consciousness, he couldn't remember what had happened after that point. In any case, he'd collapsed the second he walked into his son's dorm.

When he woke up he was surrounded by his son and his son's college friends. There was a piss stain on his crotch, and he looked up at his son, filled with embarrassment and remorse. "Your dad has brought shame on you," he said. His son, his expression somewhere between tearful and delighted, replied, "Don't worry, Dad. You didn't harm our national pride in public—I couldn't be more grateful."

3

RALO

One

Setting down this blank page before me to write the story of Ralo is not a pleasant task. As soon as I think of him, that thick yellow snot hanging from his nose starts to wave back and forth before my eyes.

Ever since Ralo came into this world, his mother was the only family he'd ever known. When he learned how to talk, some cruel men from the camp would have a laugh by asking him who his dad was. As far as Ralo was concerned, this was a question he had to put to his mother.

"Mom, who's my dad?"

"Don't ever mention that word again." His mom dealt him a slap and then squeezed him tightly to her breast. Before long, however, a man began to appear at their house in the evenings. Later on he started to visit during the day too, and eventually he simply moved in with them. "Ralo, my darling, this is your dad," his mother lovingly informed him. But, unlike the other dads in the camp, this man never gave his son a single sweet or a single kiss. On top of this, whenever Ralo came near him, he would recoil in disgust: "Hey! Look at that snot—get away from me." Ralo's snot was like running water: as soon as he wiped it away, it came flowing right back. "His brains are dripping out again," his mom always said.

Before Ralo knew it he was fourteen years old, but the snot hanging from his nose was even thicker and longer than before. By this time all the other kids his age could ride a horse and shoot a bow and arrow. He was the only one who still didn't dare ride a tame horse on his own—he had to ride in the saddle with his mother instead. "Ralo, you riding in your mom's lap again?" the others would tease him.

One morning the family was preparing to move to their winter camp. As Ralo clung to the guide rope of the yak that his stepfather was loading up, the animal started. "Hold on tight!" his stepfather said.

With a line of snot running from his nose into his mouth, Ralo grit his teeth, bit his lip, and clung to the yak for dear life.

"*Oh ya!* It's always better to have a man than a dog," said his stepfather with satisfaction. "Hold on tight, hold—" but before he could finish, the yak reared again and Ralo was tossed facedown on the ground, losing his grip on the guide rope. The old yak bolted like a thing possessed, causing the saddle to slip down to its belly. The family possessions were scattered everywhere and trampled beyond salvation.

"You're angry at the yak, but it's the horse that gets the whip," as the saying goes. The stepfather charged over in a fit of rage and screamed, "You useless little snot! Can't even hold onto a yak properly!" With that he delivered two hard slaps to Ralo's face, causing the snot on the boy's chin to drip down to his chest. "Don't you dare hit my son!" called out his mother, running over to them. "If you lay a finger on my son again . . . you won't have a home here anymore!"

"Ha! The only reason I stayed here in the first place was that I felt sorry for the two of you. I'm leaving." And his stepfather did indeed set off on his way.

"Don't let Dad leave . . ."

"Shut your dog mouth! What dad?" His mom slapped him and held him to her breast. Both mother and son burst into tears.

How many people there are in this world! But apart from his mother, Ralo didn't have a single relative, just as his mother had no one apart from Ralo. And yet, the Lord of Death had not the slightest bit of compassion for the two of them. Like a wolf pouncing into a flock of sheep, he came to pluck Ralo's mother from the multitudes of the world and lead her into the next life. Though Ralo and his mother had no family but each other, when the others in the camp heard about his mother's death, there wasn't a single dry eye. No doubt, this was out of compassion for Ralo.

Two

In the summer of the year that Ralo's mother died, a few decent folks from the camp got together and decided to send Ralo off to board at the district primary school. In reality, this was not so much in order for him to learn to read and write as it was to put a roof over his head.

As it happened, I started school that same year, so Ralo and I became classmates. But Ralo was five years older than I—in fact, he was older than everyone else in the class.

At first, Ralo was a great student. He memorized the thirty letters of the alphabet before any of the other students in the class, causing the teacher to declare, "Everyone should learn from Ralo." However, a few days later when the teacher asked us to write each letter on the board, Ralo couldn't even write the first one, reducing the class to hysterics. "No one should learn from Ralo," the teacher said.

"No one should learn from Ralo." This phrase spread through-out the school.

It turned out that we really shouldn't learn from Ralo. By the time we moved up to the next grade, Ralo still couldn't write the alphabet, so he was terrible at his studies; he had snot constantly dripping from his nose, so his hygiene was terrible; and he was always smoking, so he was terrible at following the rules. In the end, he was held back. But as far as Ralo was concerned, none of this was anything to be worried about because there was no one who would reproach him for it. The main things Ralo cared about were where he would stay for the summer holidays and how he was going to get cigarettes once all the teachers and students had gone home. As it was, Ralo got all his cigarettes in exchange for cleaning the teachers' houses, washing clothes and getting food for the older students, and subbing for his classmates when it was their turn to tidy up the classroom.

Students from nomad areas had a bad habit of not coming back on time for the start of the term. At the end of the summer and winter holidays there was often a delay of five or six days before classes could begin in earnest. Ralo, however, never once took leave to go back home, and moreover he always arrived at school before the new term even began. On this point, every-one really should have learned from Ralo.

A few fights are always going to break out in any school, and ours was no exception. Some of the troublemakers would delib-erately shout, "No one should learn from Ralo!" within his ear-shot. Ralo would chase them madly, but if one stopped to face him and looked like he was up for a fight, Ralo would say, "Teacher said I'm not allowed to fight," and like that his nerve would be gone. But as soon as the boy turned to leave, Ralo would pursue him once again, butting him with his shoulder and demanding to know, "Why shouldn't you learn from me?" One day, a student seven years younger than Ralo shoved him to the ground and jumped on his back. "Look how fast my horse is!" the boy yelled, bouncing on Ralo and pretending to ride him. "Ah—Teacher . . ." cried Ralo, his flowing tears mixing with his snot, which in turn glued together with the dirt on his face. No matter how much he bucked, he couldn't shake the boy. From that point on, everyone knew that Ralo might be big physically, but he didn't have an ounce of strength. And so the bullies multiplied.

When we moved up a grade for the second time, Ralo could just barely recognize the thirty letters of the alphabet and still couldn't write any of them, so he was held back again. The third and fourth years were the same. But whenever the teachers needed a sheep slaughtered, Ralo was indispensable, so it seemed that there wasn't any harm in keeping him back.

At the end of the fifth year I finished primary school and moved to the County Nationalities Middle School.

Three

One morning in the middle of winter, as a typical snowstorm of the northwest highlands was dancing in the sky, I was in my office stoking a fire in the stove.

Suddenly, a nomad charged in without even knocking. "Is this the People's Court?"

"Yes, can I help you with something?"

"Well, well! Aren't you Döndrup?"

"Yes, and you . . ."

"Don't act like you don't know me!" He dragged a stool over to the stove and sat himself down. "You become a cadre and you forget your old classmates, is that it?"

Wait, was this Ralo, my classmate from ten years ago? *Ah tsi,* he really had aged. His forehead was lined with wrinkles and a cluster of uneven whiskers had sprouted about his mouth. What hadn't changed was the thick yellow snot coming from his nose.

"Ah, well, of course I know you. Is something the matter?"

"Of course something's the matter!" Ralo sucked in his snot before continuing. "Someone stole my wife. He's called Sönam Dargyé. He's the most no-good man in the camp. If you don't believe me, just go down to Drakmar Camp—ask anyone there, and they'll tell you the same. Last year the bastard stole Aku Rapgyé's horse, and this year he sold Ané Tsokyi's old *dzo* to some Muslim! And then yesterday, he beats me up and steals my wife, like it's nothing. Doesn't your court have the power to punish him, or are you afraid of him? Is your People's Court going to help Ralo the proletarian, or aren't you? I want to know today!" As Ralo went on and on, the snot ran down to his chin.

"Of course you'll get help, but this is the criminal court. You need to take your case to the civil court."

"I don't understand this criminal civil stuff." Ralo was getting angry. "If you're not afraid of Sönam Dargyé, then go arrest him and get my wife back! Come to think of it, you can arrest her too while you're at it."

"Don't get all worked up." I passed Ralo a cigarette. "Ralo, my old classmate. We haven't seen each other in years. How about we catch up first? What have you been up to all this time?"

"Okay. All right then." Ralo gradually calmed down and we started to talk.

What follows is a few events that had occurred in Ralo's life since we parted ways. In order to give the story its own flavor, I've done a bit of adding and subtracting here and there, but apart from that it's mostly all the truth—in this, dear readers, you can trust me.

Four

Although Ralo still couldn't write the alphabet, he had grown older than most of the teachers at the school and there was just no way he could stay on, so in the end he was expelled. The reason given was that he had knocked on a female teacher's door one night. With no home and no family, what choice did Ralo have but to become a drifter?

At first, Ralo staved off the cold and hunger by stopping at any house he came across and volunteering to do manual work or put the cattle out to pasture. Once, an old man at one of these houses thought, Eh, *it's about time for our daughter to get a husband. This drifter Ralo can't control his snot, but he's not a bad herder, and at least he doesn't have sticky fingers. If we get him as our son-in-law, we won't have to get any betrothal gifts, either. Not bad!*

For Ralo, this was most welcome indeed.

The strange thing was that Ralo, as if he'd been possessed, soon stopped doing any work at all, and wouldn't even go graze the cattle. "I'm your son-in-law, not your slave," he would say. This infuriated the old man. "Gah! The ingratitude of it! If I don't teach that snot-nosed bum one hell of a lesson, then I'm no man!" Ralo paid the old man no mind and carried on doing whatever he pleased. Though there was nothing he could do about the snot, his cracked lips seemed to be healing and his face began to emit a red glow. Every day he combed his short, fine marmot-tail braid, and he drew out his speech in a slow drawl: "Ah ..." "Oh ..." "Really ..." "Strange ..." "I've never heard that before ..." "There's an old saying. ..." You'd never have thought that this was the same man who'd been a snot-nosed drifter only a few days before.

But how could Ralo know that "one hell of a lesson" awaited him?

For a few days, the family had been stockpiling beer, cigarettes, and sweets, making bread, and slaughtering sheep and cows, as if they were preparing for a grand celebration. When Ralo asked what was going on, they said that a great lama was coming to visit.

"Oh, what good fortune for us!" said Ralo, combing his braid.

Ralo had a habit of getting out of bed very late in the morning. That day being no exception, it was almost midday before he was up. Putting on his fur-lined coat and exiting the tent, he saw a great many horses tied up outside and heard the sounds of raucous laughter and singing. Thinking to himself that the lama had arrived, he immediately fastened his belt and rushed over, but on entering the other tent he found everyone staring at him curiously. Puzzled, Ralo looked about and discovered his wife, decked out in her finest splendor, kneeling next to another young man. "What's all this?" he demanded, even more puzzled now.

"Our family is getting a son-in-law," his wife's younger brother replied.

"Who are we getting a son-in-law for?"

"My sister, who else? He's not for me." Everyone burst out laughing.

"Is having two husbands allowed?"

"What? What two husbands?"

"Me, him."

"Ha ha ha! A snotty little bum like you who gets drunk without even drinking? You're the family's sheep herder, how could you be her husband?"

"This is impossible! You can't insult someone like this! If I don't die right here in front of you, then I'm no man!" Ralo brandished his fists and leaped forward as the crowd struggled to restrain him. "You can't stop a mad dog, and you can't restrain a madman," as the saying goes, and Ralo worked himself up into an even greater frenzy. "Haha! Have you never heard of the royal genealogies of the Ralo family? I come from a line of kings and queens! If I don't bathe this camp in blood today, then my name's not Ralo! I'm Ralo, you . . ." Ralo ranted on and on until the snot running into his mouth finally brought him to a halt.

The crowd, moved to hysterics by this absurd scene, let him go. Ralo didn't dare raise his fists to the brother, so he just butted him a bit with his shoulder. "It's my sister's wedding day, so I'm not getting in a fight with a snotty little bum like you. Get a grip on yourself and piss off back to wherever you came from," said the younger brother. But Ralo simply wouldn't leave him alone and continued to butt him with his shoulder until the brother, his patience exhausted, grabbed Ralo's braid and tossed him to the floor, pulling out the braid at the roots as he did so.

"*Ah ho*, my braid! It's worth a whole yak . . ." Ralo rolled about on the floor in a fit. "If you don't repay me for my braid then I'm not going anywhere!"

"If you don't leave I'll cut your ear off." Unsheathing his knife, the brother stepped toward him. Ralo jumped to his feet and ran like the wind.

Five

Ralo wasn't worried at all about his wife getting married to someone else. What he was worried about was how he could face other people without his beautiful braid. But before long his stomach was empty, and he had no choice but to return to civilization once more.

Ralo passed through many different camps and stayed at many different houses. At first, he would volunteer to do manual work or put the cattle out to pasture at any house he came across. But as soon as his belly was full, he'd give up his herding duties and start talking with that slow drawl: "Ah . . ." "Oh . . ." "There's an old saying. . . ." Some houses kicked him out with a "Get lost," while others he left of his own accord.

One day Ralo arrived at a monastery. As the monastery was in the process of being rebuilt, it just so happened that they were taking in monks.

There was never any point in drifting through the mundane world anyway, and since that asshole cut off my precious braid, I've really got no way to face people. I might as well become a monk; that way I can at least chant some scriptures for my dear old mom. With these thoughts in mind, Ralo shed his lay clothing and adopted the robes of a monk, taking as his Dharma name "Chöying Drakpa."

Chöying Drakpa didn't miss a single assembly, and he memorized the Refuge Vows and other elementary chants before any of the other monks. *This chanting scriptures business is much easier than what we did in school. This is my kind of studying!* he thought. His continued devotion to his studies earned him the repeated praise of the disciplinarian, praise that almost reached the level of that phrase from his youth: "Everyone should learn from Ralo."

But gradually Chöying Drakpa came to know of the "secret activities" and "open deeds" of certain lamas and monks. *If that's the way it is, then what's the point?* he thought. From then on, he was only at the monastery if there was something to eat and drink, or if there were families of the deceased offering donations to the monks. The rest of the time he spent in the nearby town watching movies, smoking cigarettes, and even drinking beer (which he called "fruit juice"), and so that other phrase from his youth once again reared its head: "No one should learn from Ralo."

Worse than that, one afternoon a rumor blew through the monastery that Chöying Drakpa had been chasing after a girl from the camp across the river. Soon this rumor also reached the ears of the disciplinarian and some of the old monks. *Chöying Drakpa might be lazy,* thought the disciplinarian, *but he has renounced worldly existence and turned his mind to the sacred Dharma, so there's no way he could get up to such shameless things. Perhaps it's nothing but lies and slander. I'll believe it when I see it with my own eyes!*

But there were two monks who did indeed see it with their own eyes. Chöying Drakpa, finding himself at loose ends, had gone down to the banks of the Tsechu to drink a "fruit juice." It was a summer afternoon and the rays of the midday sun were streaming

over Tsezhung County. Amid the soft green grass of the highlands great bouquets of globeflowers were blooming—from a
distance it looked just like someone had laid out a green carpet
dotted with yellow. Through this whole scene the Tsechu River
flowed gently. If anyone with even a single artistic bone in their
body were to come here, then the strains of "The Blue Danube"
would naturally drift into their ears, as no matter what angle you
looked at it from, the Tsechu really was just as lovely as the beautiful Danube.

Just then a girl from the camp across the river came to fetch
water. She truly was a beauty. As she drew water she cast a glance
at Chöying Drakpa from the corner of her eye, and he fell like an
animal into a trap. *At the end of the day, the most beautiful thing in
the world is a woman*, he thought. Seized with a sudden impulse,
he struck up a Malho love song:

> Can a wild yak climb
> on the misty mountain?
> Can a little goldfish swim
> in the emerald lake?
> Can I have the company
> of the enchanting girl?

Without giving it much thought, the water-fetching girl
responded with her own Ganlho song:

> A black cloud with yellow rim
> is made up of frost and hail;
> a monk neither clergy nor lay
> is the foe of Buddhist ways.

Because she sang quickly, Chöying Drakpa didn't quite get the
gist of the song, nor did he stop to give it much consideration.

Usually it's pretty rare for girls to sing to boys, he thought, *but this one replied to me straight away. She must be into me!* Overcome with joy and completely forgetting both the disciplinarian and his vows, he plowed into the Tsechu without even taking his off his boots.

At first, the girl thought the monk was just kidding around with her, so she wanted to kid around with him, but when she saw Chöying Drakpa rushing toward her, boots still on and snot running down to his chin, she thought, *This monk must be crazy!* Throwing aside her water bucket, she fled in terror.

When they witnessed this farcical scene, the monks who had been studying by the river couldn't help but burst into laughter. At that moment, Chöying Drakpa came to his senses and stood, dazed, in the middle of the river.

Six

The sun set, and the monastery became even more still and peaceful.

"The greatest burden in the world isn't having work to do, but having nothing to do"—what an accurate statement. It was indeed as if Chöying Drakpa was suffering under the weight of having nothing to do. He got up late in the morning and couldn't get to sleep at night. The water-fetching girl's alluring features and that sidelong glance (which he took as flirtatious) refused to disappear from his mind. Heaving a sigh, he left his monk's quarters.

The curved sickle moon hung in the southwestern sky like an old man leaning on his walking stick. The sound of dogs barking drifted over from the camp on the other side of the Tsechu, and looking in that direction, Chöying Drakpa could see each of the homes clearly. One place had a fire going in the stove, and he could see it even more clearly than the others.

The face of the water-fetching girl appeared before Chöying Drakpa's eyes like a film projected on the screen of his mind. He returned to his room, took off his monk's robes, and put on his old fur-lined coat.

It was just over a mile from the monastery to the camp across the river, so Chöying Drakpa arrived there in no time at all. He turned toward the home with the blazing lamplight, and tiptoeing up to the flap of the tent he peeked inside, but only one person was in there. It was a woman, but sadly it wasn't the water-fetching girl. She was sitting by the stove with her head in her hands, as though something was weighing on her mind.

Chöying Drakpa forgot about the water-fetching girl entirely and couldn't help but enter the tent. The woman jumped up in fright, an "*Ah ma!*" escaping her mouth. After a moment she calmed down and asked who he was.

"I'm a passerby," Chöying Drakpa answered with a grin. "Can I stay the night here?"

The woman sized up Chöying Drakpa in detail. He was tall and skinny with thick eyebrows and a purplish complexion.

"*Ah tsi*, of course you can." She got up, and with a smile poured Chöying Drakpa a cup of tea. "Have a seat on the mat."

Chöying Drakpa took a seat and examined his surroundings, and gradually his gaze came to rest on the woman. She was around thirty, with dark red cheeks and a high nose. She was plump and had a bulging chest. Chöying Drakpa felt his skin tingle with desire. "Is it just you here?" he asked her, flushing.

"*Eh* . . ." she sighed, a forlorn expression appearing on her face. "I had a good-for-nothing husband, but he left me and ran off to become a monk."

"Ah, how terrible! Most monks are shameless like that. I can't stand monks."

"Absolutely. There's no one in the world who loves to eat and hates to work more than a monk."

"Rubbish!"

"Huh?"

"Oh—I mean those monks love to talk rubbish too."

"Do you smoke?" the woman asked.

"Of course not . . . oh . . . yes, I do, I do."

"Give me one, would you? This loneliness has made me take it up."

After expounding for a while on the joys and benefits of smoking, Chöying Drakpa fished around in his pocket. "Oh—too bad! I didn't bring any today."

Chöying Drakpa and the woman talked for some time, and now and then he would send some compliments her way. After a while their intentions began to align.

"Ah, 'There's no suffering in the recitation hall, but you have to sit 'til your butt's numb, and there's no happiness in samsara, but you can still dispel your troubles'—what a true saying!"

"What? You've been in a recitation hall?"

"I was before; it was pointless. What if the two of us could be together our whole lives, wouldn't that be great?"

"If that's what you want, then it's easily done."

"Of course that's what I want! But we can't stay here, because . . ." Chöying Drakpa recounted all of his troubles to her. After hiding out at her place for a few days, he helped her gather up all of her necessities, and under the cover of the moonlight they headed for Chöying Drakpa's hometown.

Seven

When Chöying Drakpa was a monk, if someone called him Ralo instead of Chöying Drakpa he would get angry and butt them with his shoulder. Now that he had returned home, people once again called him Ralo and he seemed to like it, so we'll go back to calling him Ralo too.

Ralo's household registration was still here in the area, and his mother's nomad tent and her belongings had been left in the camp storehouse. The Nomad Committee gave him a relief stipend and gathered some sheep and cattle from the community for him to tend, for which he had to sign a contract. At first Ralo worked diligently and his house really seemed like a home, but as soon as he had clothes on his back and food in his belly, the seeds of laziness gradually sprouted again. He stopped tending the livestock, stopped working, and went into town to idle around. Eventually his livestock contract was rescinded, and his wife lost all patience with him.

Ralo had been in town for a few days, and after his money had all dried up he returned home to discover that his wife was nowhere to be seen. According to his neighbors, she'd been taken away by Sönam Dargyé, so off he went to Sönam Dargyé's house to fetch her back.

"This is my home now," she said.

"*Ah tsi*, are you possessed or what?"

"You're the one who's possessed!" Sönam Dargyé approached him. "She's my legal wife, what other home has she got except this one?"

Ralo, incensed, started to butt Sönam Dargyé with his shoulder. "You'll steal someone's wife in broad daylight?!"

"If you think I stole her, then go report it to the police. Then we'll see whose wife she is."

Only then did Ralo remember that there is a place that can subdue tyrants and protect the weak: a place they call "the courthouse."

Eight

I took Ralo to the civil court and introduced him, then went back to the office.

The civil court summoned Sönam Dargyé and the woman to investigate the matter. "It's true that Ralo and I lived together for a while," she said, "but we weren't husband and wife. If he says we were, then where's the marriage certificate? Isn't it against the law to live together without a marriage certificate? So my marriage to Sönam Dargyé is completely legal." She produced a marriage certificate from her pocket.

According to the verdict of the court, the woman was Sönam Dargyé's legal spouse. Ralo's lawsuit had about as much impact as throwing a stone into Qinghai Lake.

Ralo now finally realized the importance of getting a marriage certificate. He felt a deep sense of regret that he hadn't sorted out this marriage certificate thing before. He gave himself a slap on the face, and the snot ran down to his chin.

Nine

Ralo exited the courthouse and wandered aimlessly down the street. Coming to the door of a restaurant, he realized that he hadn't had breakfast or lunch yet. He felt a wave of heat in his stomach, which emitted a long rumble. Unable to stop himself, he went into the restaurant, but unfortunately he didn't have a penny to his name.

A lot of kids these days will eat without paying for it, but Ralo was not that kind of person—in fact, there was one time he returned four thousand yuan he found on the street straight to its owner without a moment's hesitation. No one could accuse Ralo of having sticky fingers, unless they were talking about him picking cigarette butts out of the teachers' trash back when he was in school.

Ralo stood in a daze, staring at the mouths of the diners. As he stared he found himself thinking back to his time as a monk: the faithful masses would always donate congee filled with more meat than rice, and there would even be raisins and sugar. If ever a family that wasn't so well off substituted dates for raisins, the monks would very likely say, "Hey, they've put damn dates in here!" and with no hesitation at all upend their bowls on the table.

I really didn't know the value of food in those days, he thought, sighing. Ralo swallowed a mouthful of saliva and turned to leave, but his stomach continued to emit the warning sign that he had to eat something.

Ah—what can I do? I've got to get some food, no matter what! Ralo cast about desperately for a familiar face. *In the old days*, he thought, *I'd sell a sheep or a cow and drink to my heart's content, then all my classmates and people I knew would be buzzing around me like bees. Where have all those people gone now?* His thoughts turned to the old yak, the one he used to ride. That yak was the only one from his herd of livestock worth any money, as well as his only means of getting around. But what's more important than your stomach? Don't all living things, from the lowest ant to the noblest human, rush about madly just for the sake of their stomachs?

Ralo sold that old yak for seven hundred yuan. If he'd been an experienced trader, there's no doubt he could have got more for it. But as far as Ralo was concerned, that was a most satisfactory sum, as never before in his life had he held so much money in his hands.

Ten

"I'm Ralo, and I'm rolling in it! Drink, drink, drink . . ." Ralo was a little bit drunk. He was in a restaurant, waving a handful of hundred-yuan bills in the air and drinking beer in the middle of a crowd. "As for Ralo's paternal ancestry and maternal ancestry . . ." he began, snot running down to his chin.

It was dusk, and the restaurant was lit up. A woman kept peeking in through the doorway and looking around. As Ralo was coming back from taking a piss, he saw her and stayed outside for a moment to size her up. From the look of her clothes, she wasn't a local.

"Where are you from?" asked Ralo, staring at her.

"Amchok," said the woman, turning around to look at Ralo. She was just over twenty years old, her clothes were worn out, and she had cracked lips, but her deep-set eyes gave off a sincerity and a purity that called to Ralo's mind the image of the water-fetching girl from the year before.

"Have you ever been to the Tsechu to fetch water?"

Not understanding the meaning behind his question, she stared at him in bemusement.

"You've definitely been to the Tsechu to fetch water." Ralo continued to interrogate her as though he were a policeman. "What are you doing here?"

"I want to eat something . . . but . . ."

Ralo realized that she must have no money. "I know you. I've seen you before. Just wait a second." He went into the restaurant and whispered a few words to a young man who had the appearance of an official. The man passed him a key, and he returned. "Come on, let's go eat."

The woman was hesitant and stayed where she was. "Don't be afraid," said Ralo. "I know you." He tugged on her sleeve and she somewhat reluctantly went along.

Side by side, they went into a narrow alley.

"There's no happiness in samsara, but you can dispel your troubles!" blurted out Ralo. On top of the proverb, he added: "Let's get a marriage certificate."

"*Ah tsi!* What are you talking about? I've got a husband."

"Ah, but after we get a marriage certificate, you'll be my legal wife. Then no one can interfere, whether you had a husband before or not!"

"Really?"

"Really! I had a wife before too, but she got a marriage certificate with some other guy so the court said she wasn't my wife, but the other guy's wife. 'Chinese rely on writing, Tibetans rely on their word,' as they say."

"Then it's up to you. I can't get along with him anyway. If I could, then what would I be doing all the way out here, wandering around on my own?"

The strange thing was that, in this place, it was hard to get divorced but there were no procedural requirements at all for getting married. As long as both parties consented, that was it. So Ralo and this virtual stranger went down to the county government and got a marriage certificate, no problem.

Though there was no way that she could be the water-fetching girl, compared to the yellow-toothed wife—or partner—he'd had before, she was prettier and a whole lot nicer. So Ralo swore from the bottom of his heart that he would change his bad and idle ways and resolved to spend his days with this honest woman. He even swore off the drink before a lama.

Ralo genuinely fell in love with her. This love was something he hadn't felt at all with the previous two women. For instance, when he went to the county seat to buy grain, he wouldn't waste a single second messing around and would hurry back as soon as possible with a new shirt or some sweets for his wife. And as soon as she saw Ralo coming back in the distance, she would rush out the mile or so to meet him, bringing food and drink with her. Things were going well for the two of them. They used the old tent that Ralo's mother had left behind to store dung, and the brand-new one they moved into was filled with the sound of laughter.

Eleven

Some people said that this woman put Ralo on the straight and narrow. Others even said that she might be the reincarnation of

Ralo's mother. Either way, ever since they'd been together Ralo really had become a different person. There was even less snot on his upper lip than there used to be.

However, one day, two men from the Public Security Bureau showed up completely out of the blue and took Ralo and his wife away to the county seat.

According to the court, his wife had committed bigamy, so she was sentenced to six months in prison. Ralo cried until the tears and snot mingled on his chin. Coming up close to him, she said, "Ralo, don't lose heart. Six months isn't that long. I'll always be yours."

What sincere and kind words! These words gave Ralo a kind of courage and hope that he had never felt before. Wiping away the snot and the tears, he stood up straight and called out, "Don't worry, I'll wait for you!"

PART II

Twelve

I wrote the story of Ralo in 1988, and it was published in *Light Rain* magazine in 1991. In the autumn of 1992 I was working in a small town about thirteen miles from the county seat. Once, when I was drunk out of my mind, a colleague took the opportunity to phone the county police with a false accusation against me and I was put in jail. For a writer like me, this seemed like a heaven-sent opportunity to experience prison life, something you wouldn't come across in a hundred years, and it also seemed like it had been arranged especially for me to write the end of "Ralo."

When I awoke, or rather when I sobered up, it was already light, and only then did I realize that I was in jail. The other prisoners gathered around me, and before long prisoners from other cells also arrived, like vultures landing on a corpse. One after the other they came up to ask me why I'd been "invited" here. Later I discovered that when a new prisoner arrived, the older prisoners would come surround him and press him with all manner of questions, regardless of what ethnicity he was or whether they knew him or not. This wasn't really out of concern for him, it was more a way of passing the time. Unfortunately I was a great disappointment to them, as not only did I have no idea why I'd been "invited" here, I couldn't even say how I'd been "invited." They left, feeling very let down. Thinking about it now, I realize this must have been the first time they'd ever met someone who had no idea why or how he'd been "invited," and they probably thought it bizarre or hilarious, which I suppose had to count as their entertainment for that day.

Ralo loitered by my side. "Yeah, you were wasted when they brought you in last night," he said. He lowered his head, revealing that braid like a marmot's tail.

Ralo's braid had completely lost its luster, like a tattered rope left for years in a pile of manure. On top of that, it was filled with lice and lice eggs, making it look gray, as though covered in yogurt. Some of these lice were alive and some were dead, and some it was hard to tell. "Lice as big as yaks," as people fond of exaggerating would say; or "as many lice eggs as atoms," as those of a more scientific bent would have it. If Ralo's head had been the earth, then the lice and their eggs would have been like humankind— each one extracting nutrients in accordance with its relative strength and intelligence. Ralo's brother-in-law had once pulled out the braid at the root and left him with no way to face people. But how true that Chinese proverb is, "If the old doesn't go, the new won't come": Ralo's braid had now grown even thicker and longer than before.

The editor of *Light Rain* kept urging me to continue the story of Ralo and see it through to its conclusion. He even expressed the hope that the spring wind of Reform and Opening Up could transform Ralo into a successful entrepreneur or a wealthy businessman or something. Either way, he wanted me to present the readers with a new kind of man. What a rare thing that is these days—I could dash off something without even thinking about it and get a paycheck. But in reality, no matter how that spring wind of Reform and Opening Up blew, it wasn't going to turn Ralo into a successful entrepreneur, and it wasn't going to turn him into a wealthy businessman either. I'd heard that Ralo had become an accomplished practitioner who subdued many demons. Some said that Ralo had become a master of divination with a flawless awareness of the past, present, and future, and moreover that he'd determined that his mother had been reincarnated as a dog, and he brought that dog home and kept it on a diet of meat and milk. In Drakmar Township the district head allegedly declared that their primary development target was to bring the living standards of the township's residents up to the level of Ralo's mother/dog by the year 2000. I'd heard these and other incredible stories but didn't believe a word of them, so I never bothered to check their veracity with Ralo. Our unexpected meeting here was, therefore, a heaven-sent stroke of good fortune, but I felt that this opportunity would be short-lived, as in my mind I was positive that at any moment a policeman would arrive and say, "Comrade Döndrup, I'm very sorry. You can go now."

"The cops brought you in by your arms and legs, holding your head up," Ralo continued. "At first we thought it was the body of a prisoner who'd killed himself, and they were putting it in our cell temporarily. It was scary. Later on I realized it was you, and I thought when you woke up we'd talk. I waited for ages, but you didn't wake up.

"*Eh*—drinking's really bad for you. You don't even know what you're in for." As he spoke, Ralo shook his head, giving the impression that he'd grown much wiser. Judging from the fact that he no longer drew out his speech in a slow drawl—"Oh . . . really," "There's an old saying . . ." and the like—you could tell that he'd fallen on hard times, or at least that he was feeling low.

"*Eh*—maybe you didn't actually do anything wrong." Ralo scratched his head repeatedly. "'Cos—I swear to Alak Drong—I'm not a thief either, but they still brought me here." As he spoke he discovered two yak-sized lice struggling for all they were worth between his long fingernails. With the practiced and nimble movements of a monkey Ralo tossed the lice into his mouth, and two crisp and clear crunches rang through the room. A few days later, when Ralo took off his fur jacket, laid it on the ground, and began popping lice into his mouth like peas, I told him to knock it off. "Lice blood won't fill the belly, but the crunching will please the ear," he said, which is true, I suppose. The weather that day was lovely, and for some unknown reason Ralo was also in a great mood. Our belts and shoelaces had all been confiscated, meaning there wasn't much we could do but hold up our trousers with our left hands. Ralo likewise held up his trousers with his left hand, and with his right he laid out his fur jacket and sunbathed for a spell. The army of lice emerged like mushrooms sprouting after rain and began to dance about on the tips of the jacket's hairs. By a common impulse the other prisoners gathered around Ralo's jacket, shouting "Over there! Over here!" as they pointed and grabbed at the lice. "Don't rush—don't rush—" said Ralo calmly in the manner of a general returning triumphantly from battle. He picked out the largest lice and ate them, a sight that made the roots of my teeth itch. "Hey, Ralo, don't do that," I protested. "There's an old saying—'Lice blood won't fill the belly, but the crunching will please the ear,'" he responded, and began to pluck the lice from the others' hands and toss them into his mouth with a *crunch*. He had the look of a man enjoying his fill of an inexhaustible supply of riches.

Thirteen

With a piercing metallic clank the cell door swung open, and the guard and cook came in bearing food. There was a large plate of mutton *momos* sent by my family, as well as some toiletries. "Is there anything else you need them to bring?" they asked.

"No, nothing. I'll be out soon."

"I don't want to disappoint you, but you won't be getting out today, at any rate."

"Then tell them to bring a book."

"I'm afraid you're only allowed to read books about law."

"That's fine," I said, thinking that I would write down the name of a book for him, but when I put my hand in my pocket I discovered that I didn't have a pen or a notebook—not even a piece of paper. Seeing my confusion, the guard placed his pen and a piece of paper in my hand. "Your things are all being kept for you," he explained.

"And ask them to bring some cigarettes," I added as the guard was leaving.

Ralo came over to me. "Looks like the warden's being good to you. Do you know him?"

"Everyone knows everyone in a little town like this. Besides, I used to run into him all the time back when I was a public defender. Why, does he treat you badly?"

"No, no. It's the other guard who's hard on us. He's a real son of a bitch. Calls me 'snotnose'—the guy has a serious attitude problem. This guard treats us okay, but there's no way he'd give me a piece of paper and a pen and let me write a letter home. *Eh*— it really helps to know Chinese."

The food in jail couldn't compare to my mutton *momos*, so I told Ralo to share them with me. I'm not sure why, but I used to think that fat people could put more away and that the fatter you were, the more you could eat, but I was completely wrong—or at least I guess you could say that that day provided some proof that skinny people can put it away too: by the time I'd eaten two or three *momos*, Ralo had polished off the entire plate.

"Maybe you didn't actually do anything wrong, just like how I never stole that horse—swear to Alak Drong. But they still brought me here, didn't they?" I don't know if it was by way of thanks for the *momos* or if he was trying to get on my good side, but either way, he said this to me again. I thought that Ralo probably had been framed. As I heard it, the sole basis on which Ralo was accused was that he'd once invited Alak Drong to his house, and as he was accompanying him out, Ralo had said, "*Ah la la!* Machu horses really are a rare breed. I'd swap my wife to get my hands on a horse like that." That was it.

When I asked Ralo if that's how it happened, he said, "That's exactly what happened." That was the first time that Alak Drong had graced Ralo's home with his presence, and Ralo was so happy he had no idea what he was saying.

"There's an old saying—" now that Ralo was full of *momos*, he once again drew out his speech in a slow drawl "—'When nothing's going your way, you take a piss and it runs down your thigh'— how true that is. After Alak Drong left my house that time, a friend from Gansu came over. That evening he said he wanted me to accompany him to a girlfriend's place. As we were passing by Tsezhung Monastery we came across two guys from my camp looking for their cattle. After I took my friend to the edge of that cursed woman's camp, I went straight home. So the police said that I'd been to the monastery in the middle of the night and that I'd been up to something, and they took me in. No matter how much I swore I hadn't, they wouldn't believe me. Think about it—'a dog won't swallow metal and a man won't swallow his oath'—could a braided, black-headed Tibetan like me swallow an oath?"

At that moment the guard came back with a book, a few packs of cigarettes, and a thermos of milk tea. Ralo and I sat together drinking the tea and smoking the cigarettes. "*Eh*—my wife hasn't been to see me in over ten days, what's going on? Did she and my son get sick? Alak Drong protect them." Gradually, Ralo fell deep into thought.

Fourteen

The walls of the cell were white and the beds and floors were all made of wooden boards, which gave the place a feeling of cleanliness, but the door was reinforced with iron plates and the little window was covered by iron bars, leaving you in no doubt that this was no ordinary room. The jail contained people who had been taken into custody by the police, prisoners who had been given a short-term sentence (less than one year) by the courts, and also people like Ralo, who were still being investigated. Their crimes varied in severity, and for some it wasn't clear if they'd committed a crime at all. Regardless, they referred to themselves unanimously as "criminals." Only if you called yourself this were you allowed in and out of the cell, and sometimes in and out of the yard.

The practice of referring to oneself with the Chinese word for "criminal" was something that Ralo had already mastered. He would face the sentry standing bolt upright, throw back his head, suck in his snot, and say, "Reporting to the class monitor! The criminal would like to enter [or 'leave']!" When he said this it sounded just like the braying of a magnificent donkey. I heard, though, that when Ralo first arrived he didn't even know the Chinese for "report," which caused him great difficulties, so much so that things sank to the level of that phrase from his youth: "No one should learn from Ralo." Countless times the class monitor (the sentry) made him stand at the foot of the wall as punishment, I heard. This was the second time since Ralo's marriage to the nice woman that things had reached the point of "No one should learn from Ralo." The first was a few years after he returned to lay life. When still a monk he'd learned to chant some sutras, and later this became an immeasurable source of wealth for him, as more and more people requested him to come and perform religious services. Unlike the monks from the monastery, Ralo didn't haggle and barter when he did these religious services; he took whatever his patron offered. Leather, sheepskin, lambskin, sheep wool, yak wool, yak down, butter, cheese, *tsampa*—Ralo would take anything. This was very convenient for people, and as Ralo's customer base grew and grew, the income of Tsezhung Monastery's monks shrank and shrank, causing Alak Drong to become concerned. But Ralo gradually became as if possessed, or perhaps we should say his old affliction returned. When he was doing divinations he would say things like, "If you don't recite the *Hayagrīva Mantra* ten million times, then your daughter can't be saved," or "If you don't recite the *Sitātapatrā Mantra* ten thousand times, this task cannot be accomplished." Sometimes he didn't even bother with a divination, he just sat with his eyes closed for a moment, then

said, "Oh—the horse that you lost can be found to the west," or
"Your child is now in India," or "This patient only has three days
left to live—*om mani padme hum.*" For a short time Ralo was
renowned as a clairvoyant. Unfortunately, Alak Drong soon
announced: "Ralo's visions and trances are nothing but a scam."
From then on no one invited Ralo to their home to perform religious services, and he was once more reduced to the level of "No
one should learn from Ralo."

"This is all because the monks from Tsezhung Monastery are
jealous and like to lie and badmouth people," said Ralo despondently.

Though Ralo was sometimes in danger of letting that "old
affliction" flare up again, thanks to his kindhearted wife he had
undergone a sea change. He had become father to a son and was
now a livestock herder, and he spent his days happily combing
his braid. One day he invited Alak Drong to his house to present
him with a horse and two yaks. But people's jealousy is like a bad
toothache—it won't give you a moment's peace. "Haha! Even
that snotty bastard Ralo has the nerve to invite Alak Drong to
his house. Has the world gone mad?" they cried, red-eyed and
lips aquiver, and when the police came to investigate the matter
of Alak Drong's missing horse, they told them, "Who else could
it be but that snotty bastard Ralo?" and offered up some reason-
ing and evidence. "There's no response to a black lie and there's no
bottom to the black earth," as the saying goes. Ralo, slack-jawed
and nose running, could do nothing.

I couldn't help but get angry. "But that's outrageous! If you do
end up getting charged and going to court over this, then I'll
defend you." One of our cellmates, a cadre, told me that not only
had Ralo been formally charged, but also the prosecutor's office
would soon bring the case to court.

This man was called Tsepak. He was a high-level official around
forty years old. After his activities were brought to light by the
masses, the judicial authorities took him in for questioning six

times, and five of those times he'd been released without them harming a hair on his head. This time he'd come up against an anticorruption drive, and I thought he was done for sure, yet he seemed quite relaxed, as though he hadn't a care in the world. Later, after we got to know each other, I discovered the reason for this nonchalance. As he told us, quite candidly, "Look, boys, it doesn't matter if you've committed a crime or not. When you get a chance, have a word with your family and get them to take all those useless expenses and stuff them right in the judge's mouth instead. I guarantee you'll get results. If there's one thing I've learned from being both a law enforcer and a lawbreaker, it's this. I'm giving this to you straight, 'cos I feel sorry for all of you." What he meant by "useless expenses" was the money people spent on hiring top lawyers and conducting elaborate religious services. He wasn't anything like the corrupt officials of my imagination. He was refined and intelligent, skinny with a fair complexion and a pair of glasses. He looked just like a cultured intellectual. He certainly didn't give you the impression that he was a thief—at most you might think he'd pinch a couple of books. I stared at him for some time. "Akhu Tsepak, did you really pocket as much as everyone says?" I asked. "If you're on the take when no one else is then you're a fool, and if you're not on the take when everyone else is then you're even more of a fool," he said with a smile. "It's just a shame that as soon as I went on the take everyone started getting jealous and the thieves decided to catch a thief. I guess it's because when I worked for the Ministry of Justice I didn't know what I was doing and arrested too many 'thieves.' But I've stuffed money in the judges' mouths before, and I'm still stuffing, so I'll be fine."

Fifteen

The "son of a bitch" guard that Ralo mentioned finally made an appearance atop the stone wall. He had a big ass that stuck out like a black woman's, and the gun hanging at his belt made it seem to stick out even more. He strutted up and down the wall with his hands behind his back clutching a string of *mani* beads, making him look like a chicken about to lay an egg. I called him Mani Ass, and soon everyone else started calling him that behind his back too.

Mani Ass really was a son of a bitch. With the exception of Tsepak, he called us all "pricks," and Ralo he called a "snotnose prick."

"Snotnose prick, go get some water."

In his very practiced manner, Ralo held up his trousers with his left hand, grabbed the empty thermos with his right, and shuffled to the cell door. "Reporting to the class monitor! The criminal would like to leave!"

"Go."

"Reporting to the class monitor! The criminal would like . . ."

"Go."

Ralo entered bringing a thermos full of cold water and told me that it was for washing our faces the next morning.

The afternoon crept up on us and the cook arrived with some food. It was almost as if my family and Tsepak's had been in touch to arrange the perfect combination—one of us got some mutton and the other some yak yogurt.

Ralo was happy now that he had something to eat, but the food our relatives brought seemed to remind him of his own family. "My wife hasn't been in over ten days. *Ya*—she . . ." he began, but he was cut off by an interjection. "Maybe she's been snagged by someone else?"

"Hmph, this wife is nothing like that old yellow-toothed one," said Ralo with great confidence.

Out of sheer boredom the prisoners told stories from their pasts, holding nothing back. They even liked to discuss how good their women were in bed. According to Ralo, the yellow-toothed woman was peerless in that department, or at least he himself had never come across another like her. When that topic of conversation was exhausted, the braggarts and bullshitters began to invent stories. You knew it was all nonsense, but you had no choice but to listen and pretend you believed it. This was an experience that I myself was later subjected to, after we'd been through all the major things we'd seen and heard in our lives and the store of stories was empty, and we were forced to listen to the particularly skilled fabrications of one young bullshit artist. He was a half-Tibetan half-Chinese kid who'd just turned twenty. Judging from his name—Tseten Zhao—his dad must have been Chinese and his mom Tibetan. He could understand Tibetan but couldn't really speak it, so he spoke in Chinese and I translated for Ralo as I listened. He said that he'd stolen a gun from the storehouse of an army barracks and robbed a bank. He was planning to escape to Hong Kong, but he fell into the hands of the Special Forces and ended up in prison. That prison was more or less the same as this jail, he said, the only difference being that a low wall had been put across the middle, on the other side of which were the female prisoners, most of whom were fine-looking prostitutes. All it took was one glance and they'd be snuggled up to your chest. Most nights he and some of the other guys would give each other a leg up, hop the wall, and screw around with the girls.

"Didn't your prison lock the doors at night?" Ralo asked, dubiously.

"The wall around that prison was even taller than the one here. There was no way to escape even with the doors unlocked."

"Didn't the women get pregnant?"

"Yeah, many of them did."

"So who's taking care of the babies?"

"The female guards."

"Bullshit."

"*Swear on my dad's flesh.*" (This was his most accurately pronounced Tibetan phrase.)

"Okay, then tell me more!"

He knew it was a load of crap, but Ralo still preferred to listen, as it helped pass the time. Tsepak and I were reading and had no desire to listen to his made-up stories, but Ralo kept urging Tseten Zhao to continue and kept urging me to translate for him, so we were forced to do as he wished.

Since Ralo didn't wash, we took it in turns to add his water to ours; that way we got to wash our hair. This habit of washing neither his face nor his hair made the lice grow bolder, and they began to pose a threat to my well-being. Now I understood why Tsepak and Tseten Zhao had me sleep between them and Ralo. I had no choice but to suffer in silence, "like a mute eating bitter herbs," as that Chinese proverb goes. Not long after we got in bed, one of Ralo's audacious lice leaped over to my side and quite brazenly bit me in the armpit. From then on Ralo's lice began a brutal campaign of abuse against me. I warned him to get them under control, but Ralo's reaction was, to my surprise, one of indifference. "Having lots of lice means you have good karma. If they're moving onto you, you should be happy about it." Ralo's lice were now not only harming my body but also seriously harming my mental state: they grew larger overnight and turned into beasts as terrifying as crocodiles. Their long, sharp fangs first devoured Ralo; then, flashing those blood-stained gnashers, they came for me.

Completely terrified, I awoke with a scream. As Ralo snored thunderously I had a vision of the lice scraping their way along the floorboards, coming to attack me, and there was no way I could get back to sleep. Put it this way—the lice feasted on Ralo and they feasted on me, and if it weren't for the kindness of my wife bringing me clean underwear every day, who knows if I'd be here to write this story today.

Sixteen

After Tseten Zhao told us a thrilling prison break story, he feigned tiredness and pulled the covers up over his head. Then Tsepak turned in for the night, leaving me with only Ralo to talk to. After a while Ralo too went to bed, and I was kept awake by his thunderous snoring. I realized then that both Tseten Zhao and Tsepak had planned all this out in advance, their goal being to get to sleep before Ralo at all costs. It was too late for me, and I was left alone to endure the torment of Ralo's snoring and the terror of the lice. Even after I fell asleep I kept being awakened by those fearsome "crocodiles."

> With your compassion, give us your blessings
> With your love, guide us along the path
> With your wisdom, grant us accomplishments
> With your power, guide us along the path
> Dispel the outer obstacles externally
> Dispel the inner obstacles internally
> Dispel the secret obstacles into space
> With reverence, I prostrate and take refuge in you.

When I was awakened by these words, it was already light. Ralo was sitting cross-legged on his bed, palms clasped, eyes closed, chanting to himself. This scene was similar to the one I would later witness in a truck on the way to Lhasa, except on that later occasion Ralo had shaved the hair around his braid clean off, and the braid itself had been neatly plaited. But if you looked closely you could still make out several lice, maybe living, maybe not.

I hadn't actually committed a crime, but even so, during the month I was in custody my mom was so worried about me she couldn't eat during the day or sleep at night. I wanted to repay her kindness, so I asked her what I could do for her—anything you want, I said. Without thinking twice, she said she wanted me to take her to Lhasa, so that's exactly what I did. Ralo said, "When my mom passed away I couldn't even light a butter lamp for her. I've got to take my mom to see the Jowo just once while she's still alive this time, no matter what!" And like that, Ralo and I became what he called "fellow pilgrims."

Early one morning, about four, I brought my mother down to the station. The other pilgrims had long since taken their seats on the truck, and we set off accompanied by a chorus of angry grumblings from the driver about us being late.

Amid the sound of the chanting pilgrims I heard one voice that sounded very familiar to me, but I couldn't quite place it. After we'd been driving for a little while I fell asleep. It was light by the time I woke up, and it hit me then that the familiar voice was Ralo's. Like that time in the jail, he was chanting with his palms clasped and his eyes closed, and every now and then he clapped his hands together. This was what the faithful called "driving out the demons," and it gave him the appearance of a yogin.

"*Ah tsi ah tsi*, first we were classmates, then we were cellmates, and now, thanks to the Three Jewels, we're pilgrimage mates— what good fortune! Excellent, excellent." Ralo was overjoyed to discover that I was on the truck with him.

There were about fifty people on the truck, including babies so young they were still suckling at their mother's breasts and people so old they almost had the Lord of Death's noose around their necks. It was also packed with everyone's food, tents, fuel, and all the other provisions necessary for a month-long trip, as a result of which we were squeezed together so tightly that we could barely breathe. Nevertheless, with great determination, Ralo forced his way through to me, clutching a large basket to his chest with his left hand and guiding his wife by the wrist with his right. By his wife's side was a child of about five or six. He was a handsome boy who looked identical to his mother, and not a bit like Ralo. Yet, when you saw the little braid tied at the end with a woolen thread, you knew without a shadow of a doubt that this was Ralo's offspring. His name was Sangdak, but I called him "Little Ralo" for fun. If Ralo's braid was like a marmot's tail, then Little Ralo's braid was exactly like a mouse's. Ralo's wife was called Dekyi, and you could tell from a glance that she was a kind and devoted woman. With the exception of chanting, she said only one thing in the whole of the month that I spent with her: "Ralo, snot."

As Ralo smoked the cigarettes I gave him he began to talk more, and at the same time his snot drooped longer. It seemed that the more he smoked, the more his nose ran.

"Ralo, snot."

Ralo sucked in his snot and cast an angry glance at his wife, apparently in retaliation for being reprimanded in public. This habit aside, he was, in general, very good to his wife.

Seventeen

The basket that Ralo clutched at his chest contained a decrepit old dog that looked like it was on its last legs; he said it was the reincarnation of his mother. Ralo's wife had previously been sentenced for committing bigamy and had spent a few months in jail. On the night that she came back, Ralo dreamed that his mother came to his door and murmured some indistinct words, and when he got up the next morning and went outside, a puppy had appeared from somewhere. It stared at him and whined feebly, and his previous night's dream returned to his mind. There was no doubt that this was the reincarnation of his mother, he thought, and he took the dog home and fed it on a diet of meat and milk. This was the mangy dog that he now carried with him.

The dog was like many of the dogs you see in the highlands these days: a mongrel that was neither a mastiff nor a Pekingese.

It was the kind that wouldn't dare to bite a young man, but would happily ambush old folks, kids, and women. I hated that kind of dog. But Ralo called this dog "Mom," and he cherished it even more than Little Ralo, so I was forced to pretend that I liked it.

It was the first time the dog had been on a truck, and like most of the pilgrims on board, it threw up more than it ate. By the time we got to Lhasa all it could do was lie in the basket and let Ralo carry it around.

A friend from Lhasa got in touch and insisted that we go for dinner, so one night he took Ralo and me to a restaurant. At the entrance, we were greeted by a young woman who, like it says in that Tibetan love song, "from the side was like a slim bamboo, from the front was like the moon on the fifteenth." The whole time she stood by our table, refilling our tea and liquor with a smile. Ralo didn't touch the booze but he still got drunk, and with a magnanimous air produced a one hundred-yuan note. I shot him a glance to make him put it away.

If Ralo were the introspective type, he'd no doubt have remembered the wretched circumstances he faced when we were in jail. One time Mani Ass snatched away the fried dough cakes I'd given to Ralo just as he was about to eat them. "Not content with eating your own share, snotnose prick? Have to eat your friend's too? You're no different from a pig." The older prisoners said that Mani Ass stole it to feed his pigs; others said that he just ate it himself. Either way, he didn't let Ralo eat it. Ralo's eyes began to well with tears, and I felt genuinely sorry for him. The next day, I told the guard who Ralo said "treated him okay" about this incident. He apologized to us on behalf of the jail, and even said that he'd report it to the chief of the police station. Little did I expect that whenever Mani Ass was on duty after that, he'd keep Ralo and me locked up in the cell. This in turn made Ralo's lice grow especially bold, and they bit the two of us almost to death.

When it came time to pay the check, Ralo once again took out his hundred-yuan bill, but as soon as he heard the words "That'll be five hundred in total" his mouth fell open, his snot hung down, and he discreetly put it back in his pocket. Later, Ralo would often lord it over others with this: "I, Ralo, once ate a meal worth five hundred yuan!"

Though the pilgrims, who came from all sorts of backgrounds, had thousands of yuan in their pockets, spending five hundred on a single meal was, to these people, something from another world. "*Ah la la!*" exclaimed Ralo as soon as we returned to our group, "Döndrup's friend treated us to a five hundred-yuan meal! Now when I see plain old meat and butter it makes me want to throw up." Behind his back the pilgrims said, "His old affliction's back again."

Though Ralo couldn't say what he'd actually eaten at the restaurant, he maintained that "when I see plain old meat and butter it makes me want to throw up," and he didn't eat anything for five days. In the end, his face turned yellow and he fainted.

Eighteen

From the day after we arrived in Lhasa, the pilgrims spent the mornings going to the temples and the afternoons shopping. Ralo found a string of the sandalwood prayer beads he'd been wanting to buy, and when he asked how much they were, he was told ten yuan.

"Will you take eight?"

"Sure, sure."

Ralo informed his fellow pilgrims about this as though he'd discovered a new continent: "When you buy stuff you can haggle—the guy said these prayer beads cost ten yuan, but in the end I got them for only eight!" Another pilgrim produced a string of prayer beads identical to Ralo's: "This one only cost me three." Ralo's bottom lip trembled and he couldn't utter a word. A few days later, though, with an expression of eminent triumph etched on his face, he was telling that pilgrim, "I, Ralo, once ate a meal worth five hundred yuan. What's five yuan compared to that?"

On the way back from visiting Tashi Lhünpo Monastery we stopped at Samyé Monastery. At the bank of the Yarlung Tsangpo River we got on a wooden boat equipped with a tractor engine, which took half an hour to get us to the other side.

"*Ah tsi ah tsi*, this technology stuff is amazing!" Looking at the expressions of wonder on the pilgrims' faces, you could be sure they'd be telling their relatives about the marvels of this technology for years to come.

When we got to the other side of the river we came across a couple of foreign tourists. Ralo was the first to talk to them, and when I later got to know them, I found out that they were researchers from Norway studying folk customs. The husband was called Vilhelm and the wife Birna, and she could speak a bit of Chinese. Actually, rather than saying that Ralo was the first to talk to them, it would be more accurate to say that they were curious about Ralo carrying an old dog in a basket and came over to ask us about it. As soon as Birna saw Ralo she became like something possessed: "Hey, dear, come look, quick!" she yelped in English as she shot off two photos with a *click*. "Hello—" she said as she approached, her thumb sticking straight up. She shook Ralo's hand and asked him why he was carrying the dog.

The pronunciation of "hello" sounds a little bit like the Tibetan *aro*. Perhaps, in the near future, this word will be used as a kind of greeting, like *aro*. For now, at least, it didn't seem to have any derogatory or disdainful intent.[1] Birna came over to me with a "hello" and asked if I could help translate. I happily accepted and told the two of them the story of Ralo's mother/dog.

"How incredible! Absolutely wonderful. In the West it's rare to see someone take their actual mother to the hospital these days,

---

1. *Aro* is common a term of greeting in Tibetan. *Aluo*, its approximate pronunciation in Chinese, is a derogatory term used by Han Chinese to refer to Tibetans.

and he's carrying his mother's *reincarnation* around. Wow! It's really true what they say about Tibet being the last untouched holy land on earth. How incredible! Absolutely wonderful." Vilhelm was deeply moved. He didn't quite know what to do and kept on sticking his thumb up in the air. He took some colorful, expensive-looking candies from his backpack and offered them to us.

But some of the older pilgrims were displeased. "You mustn't eat the food of the heathens," they said. Another pilgrim, a cadre with Party membership, issued a solemn warning: "Be careful. They're using sugar-coated bullets to promote Peaceful Evolution."

The pilgrims didn't know what "Peaceful Evolution" meant, but they suspected it might be one of the heathens' terrifying magical powers. The elderly among them prayed to the Jowo, while the young men gripped the handles of their knives. But Little Ralo didn't understand words like "heathen," "sugar-coated bullet," or "Peaceful Evolution," so, quite unconcerned, he clutched the foreigners' hands and ate their candy.

Vilhelm and his wife had originally planned to go back to Lhasa after seeing Samyé Monastery, but they had become helplessly captivated by the Ralo family and decided to turn around and accompany us back to Samyé. They stuck their thumbs up at Ralo as they peppered him with questions and took countless photos. On the boat on the way back, Birna handed me her camera when we reached the middle of the Yarlung Tsangpo and asked me to take a picture of them with Ralo's family. I pressed the shutter, and she said "Okay" as she gave Little Ralo a kiss. After Little Ralo died, the elderly pilgrims said that it was because he'd "been contaminated by the heathens." That was the hardest time in Ralo's whole life. For days on end he sat, mouth agape, his snot running, staring into space. It was more agonizing than the death of his mother and his unjust imprisonment, even more agonizing than the time his brother-in-law ripped out his braid. And given what happened, that was completely understandable. When we were nearing home on the way back from our pilgrimage to Lhasa, Ralo was in high spirits. He kept on picking up Little Ralo and holding him out of the truck bed, saying, "Look, there's our home!" Little Ralo too was happy as a clam, his little mouse-tail braid bouncing back and forth. Right at that moment, before anyone had the chance to even register it, an oncoming truck came rushing past us like an animal leaping out of a trap and severed Little Ralo's braided head clean off, just as a child would pluck a flower from its stalk. Little Ralo's headless body continued to twitch, and the red protection cord given to him by Alak Drong before we left for Lhasa was soon dyed black by his blood.

The image of Little Ralo's tiny, innocent face still smiles in my mind, and his little mouse-tail braid still waves back and forth before my eyes.

I had become very attached to that kid while we were on the road. He charmed anyone like that, no matter who it was. In just the three or four hours we were at Samyé, Vilhelm and Birna became completely besotted with him. Just before he was beheaded, Little Ralo was asking, "Where have our yellow-haired friends gone?"

Nineteen

Tseten Zhao was eventually given a five-year sentence and taken off to prison, and our "home" suddenly felt cold and deserted. In the month or so that Ralo and I were in jail together, he did nine divinations by burning the shoulder blade of a lamb, and this was the only time he got it right. When the families of the other prisoners brought them a shoulder of lamb, Ralo saved the bones and hid them at the base of the wall. He said that when the heating stove was installed in a few days' time he could burn the shoulder blades and from the resulting markings determine whether or not we would be sentenced, and if so for how long. By the time the stove was installed Ralo had collected nine shoulder blades. Naturally, he first burned one to discover his own fate. When the dung in the furnace was burning red hot, Ralo picked up a clean shoulder blade. "I offer my prayer, I offer my tribute, I offer my veneration! Deity of Wisdom, enshroud the eyes of demons and thieves. *Ptui.*" He hocked up a ball of spit and added as an aside, "Normally I'd use a branch of cypress for benevolent spirits, but where would I get one of those? A bit of grass'll have to do." He put some grass on the shoulder blade, inserted it into the flames, and muttered some unintelligible incantations. The shoulder blade was gradually turned black by the fire, and cracks began to appear on it. Ralo sucked in his snot, retrieved the shoulder blade with his bare hands, and placed it on the ground. By this point other prisoners had gathered around the doorway of our cell, squeezing shoulder to shoulder and craning their necks to get a look. Some of the braver ones even slipped in when the watchman wasn't looking. (Whenever someone received an indictment from the prosecutor's office they would bring it to my cell straight away and gather around just like this, asking me to translate and explain it, and asking me what they should say to the court.)

Ralo spent a long while analyzing the shoulder blade, retaliating against his restless lice as he did so. "It is certain that I will not be sentenced!" he finally announced with an air of triumph.

"That's great," "That's fantastic," replied the crowd before they began inundating Ralo with requests: "Please, tell me if I'm going to get sentenced." Since this was the first time in his life he'd been so in demand, Ralo was extremely pleased, and he began to draw out his speech in a slow drawl. "*Ya*—first let me see what's going to happen with my old classmate Döndrup, then I'll check on Akhu Tsepak, *ohh*—then I'll get to the rest of you. Pass me—pass me a cigarette." In an instant, Ralo received a bounty of seven or so cigarettes, and he became even more full of himself. "*Ya*—Döndrup, Döndrup," he said, preparing to put a shoulder blade in the fire for me. "Do the others first," I said to him. "*Ohh*—that's fine," he said. "There's an old saying—'Help others achieve their goals, and your own success will follow.' *Ya*—so who's first?"

"Me!"

"Me!"

. . .

"*Ya*—" Ralo took a drag of his cigarette. "First we'll do one for Kelzang and see if we get the same result as Alak Drong," he said, inserting a bone into the flames.

This Kelzang was an incorrigible thief who'd already been arrested multiple times, and this time he'd stolen twenty-six head of cattle. I was sure he'd get at least eight years. His family, however, had sent word that "Alak Drong has performed a divination and he says there's no way you'll get sentenced, so you set your mind at ease"—and he did indeed set his mind at ease. It was unclear, therefore, if he was asking for a divination now in order to test Ralo's powers or if he was in earnest. Happily, Ralo didn't need to analyze the bone for long before he came to a conclusion. "*Ohh*—there's an old saying—you don't need to read a three-pointed bone. Not only will you not be sentenced, you'll be released soon," he declared.

"Well," said Kelzang, "this snotnose prick can't keep his snot under control, but he sure can burn a bone."

Ralo shot Kelzang an angry glare, then put some more bones in the fire. "*Ah ho!* That's no good," he exclaimed after a short interval. "Tseten Zhao will be sentenced to five years."

Thanks to these few words, in the days after Tseten Zhao was actually sentenced to five years Ralo's status rose and rose. The number of people giving him cigarettes increased, and the number of people calling him "snotnose prick" declined. Unfortunately, this bit of good fortune was very short-lived, as Kelzang ended up getting thirteen years, and shortly thereafter Ralo himself was sentenced to two. I'm sure you know very well just how devastating a situation this was for him, and just how long his snot drooped down because of it. I heard later that 60 percent of what Ralo said in court consisted of old sayings, 20 percent consisted of "In the entire family history of Ralo the proletarian no one has ever stolen anything!," and the remaining 20 percent was "I swear on the Three Jewels," "I swear on Alak Drong," and other such oaths.

Judging from the way things had been going recently, Tsepak was about done for as well. The endless supply of good food and cigarettes sent by his friends dried up all of a sudden, but more significantly, Mani Ass had changed his attitude toward him. One day he jabbed his finger at Tsepak and said, "Crooked prick! You you you . . . go get some water!"

Tsepak's mouth hung open, and it was some time before he responded. "Huh?" he said, seemingly not believing his own ears.

"Go get some water!" yelled Mani Ass.

After Tsepak came back with the thermos of water he threw himself down on the bed and closed his eyes. Ralo and I exchanged a quick glance and went over to him. "Is Mani Ass possessed today or what?" I said. Tsepak opened his eyes and sat up. "It looks like I'm really done for this time," he said.

Ralo and I stood there, not sure what to say. "Don't worry about it, boys," said Tsepak. "It's been coming. If I don't go down, then some innocent guys like you two will end up in jail. Looks like the authorities really mean to do what they say this time. Don't worry, don't worry. It's about time I reap what I sow." He suddenly seemed unburdened, like a saint awaiting the Lord of Death—a man who'd long since come to understand the principles governing the universe. From that point on, however, Mani Ass found fault with absolutely everything Tsepak did, making life unbearable for him. Out of desperation, Tsepak got a message to his family and told them to send a whole lamb to Mani Ass. For a few days after that Mani Ass's treatment of Tsepak improved considerably, but gradually he reverted to calling him "crooked prick" and finding fault where none was to be found. "I guess Mani Ass finished off the last of the lamb," said Ralo, very likely the first and only genuine truism he had uttered in his life.

Twenty

A new prisoner arrived to take Tseten Zhao's bunk. Or rather, I moved to the space next to Tsepak to avoid the incursions of Ralo's lice, and the new prisoner took my bunk. Ralo had already been sentenced, but he had a few days to appeal so he still hadn't been taken to prison. Since Tseten Zhao had left there was no one to tell Ralo any weird and wonderful stories, and since he'd been sentenced he'd also lost his appetite. But, unlike me, whether Ralo met with fortune or tragedy, he'd never ask "Why?" as he had a clear answer: "Karma." Ralo didn't know who his father was, but he must have had some ancestors at any rate, and this irrefutable logic was what they had bequeathed to him.

The new prisoner was called Damchö. He was a strongly built half-farmer half-nomad, about forty years old. Though he didn't talk about "the Special Forces" and "modernized weapons" like Tseten Zhao did, he had numerous tales of cattle and horse rustling, stretching right back to when he first learned to ride. It looked like it would be easy for Ralo to pass his last few days in jail after all. Yet it was on an evening only a few days later that Ralo, unleashing a sudden cry of "*Ah—ho—*," jumped up naked from bed, pounced on Damchö, and began to strangle him. Tsepak and I had been reading, we had no idea what the two of them had been talking about or what the problem was, and for a moment we simply looked on in bewilderment. No matter how much Damchö struggled he couldn't shake him off, and I wondered in amazement at where Ralo had got this strength. "*Ah—ho—,*" Ralo cried again, "this is for Alak Drong's horse! If I don't die right now, then I'm not a braided Tibetan! *Ah—ho—.*" Ralo pinned Damchö with his butt and gripped his throat tighter, making his eyeballs bulge so much they looked like they were going to pop out of his head. Tsepak and I leaped up and pulled at Ralo as hard as we could, but he was as immovable as a giant boulder. Damchö continued to struggle beneath him, and Tsepak and I pulled him from above. Damchö thrust out his right hand and managed to grab hold of Ralo's braid, and with one tug sent him tumbling off the bed like a sack of straw. He hopped down from the bed and delivered two sharp kicks to Ralo's chest, sending a thick string of snot drooping onto the floor. Tsepak and I moved to intervene again, but, unlike in the past, Ralo was fearless this time, pouncing toward Damchö once more with a cry of "*Ah—ho—*this is for Alak Drong's horse . . ." I managed to restrain him, and I asked him what was the matter. "The guy who stole Alak Drong's horse—it's him," he said.

"How do you know?"

"He said so himself."

Damchö did indeed admit that he was the one who had stolen Alak Drong's horse. He said that he'd straighten the whole thing out with the police first thing in the morning and tell them to release Ralo, on top of which he apologized repeatedly and said it was a great injustice if Ralo was in prison on account of this. But Ralo wasn't to be consoled. "*Ah—ho—*this is for Alak Drong's horse . . ." he cried again, doing his best to get his hands on Damchö. I had no choice but to risk a lice attack and sleep between the two of them.

The next morning Ralo sat up in bed, and when he'd finished his chanting he scratched the wall with his fingernail. Since he had no prayer beads, he put a mark like this on the wall every morning when he was done with his recitations. After he was released that afternoon I counted all the marks on the wall—there were sixty in total. This meant that Ralo had referred to himself as a "criminal" at least one hundred and eighty times.

Twenty-One

The "karma" that Ralo was always talking about continued to toy with him, treating him just like a stray dog. The terrible incident of Little Ralo's decapitation had driven Dekyi to madness. For months she tore about crying and laughing, completely uncontrollable. Finally, she jumped in a river and drowned herself.

Spring came early. The tips of countless fresh buds were poking through on the walls of the livestock enclosures and on the southern slopes of the grasslands, and the dung embankments put up by the nomad women in late autumn began to disintegrate under the warmth of the sun.

Ralo didn't get out of bed until late in the morning. He sat in the doorway of his tent sunning himself and chanting his *manis*. His chanting was different now. He no longer did it in a loud voice, and each syllable was punctuated by long pauses. Between his greasy, dirt-encrusted fingers he plied the flat sandalwood prayer beads he'd bought in Lhasa. The edges of each bead were now worn away, and they had become almost perfectly spherical. His braid had once again become a tangled lice nest, like it had been when he was in jail, and his fur jacket had torn, revealing the wool filling inside. The sight of his jacket was a painful reminder of his dear loving wife, and every time he looked at it he wept bitterly and struck himself in the chest.

Around noon his neighbors sent their kids to call Ralo for lunch. Ralo wasn't hungry in the least, and he had no desire whatsoever to see the domestic bliss of husbands with their wives and fathers with their sons. Still, he didn't have the heart to spurn the kindness of his neighbors, so he went to whichever family called him first. After his wife and son died, Ralo had given away most of his livestock to the lama and the monastery and had them perform the last rites for the departed. Now he had only five female yaks and *dzo* left, which, as he put it, were "offerings for when my mom dies." He didn't even have to worry about taking care of them, either, as he'd loaned or rented them out, along with his contracted land, to another family. In turn, this family gave Ralo and the old dog he called "Mom" yogurt and milk in the summer months and butter and cheese in the autumn. Ralo had originally been assigned this land through a drawing of lots, and it was the best piece of land in the area. For a long time after that he'd told people that he must have good karma. Now, apart from wallowing in his sorrow and chanting his *manis*, he had no obligations at all.

The weather gradually grew warmer and the nomads became busier as the days went by. It came time for them to begin storing up their butter and cheese, and there were fewer and fewer people to call Ralo over for tea. Nevertheless, one neighbor, Chaktar, tirelessly persisted in calling Ralo over to eat with his family, and he even sent his mother over to give him water and dung for fuel. Ralo was so embarrassed by this generosity that sometimes he would make his own tea and food before someone from Chaktar's family arrived. "I've just had something, I swear to Alak Drong, I swear on the Jowo in Lhasa," Ralo assured them when someone came to fetch him. Chaktar, unable to compel him, ended up giving his mother a thermos of tea and some cheese, butter, and *tsampa*, and sending her over to eat with Ralo. Chaktar's mother was called Guru Kyi. Though she was about sixty years old, her hale and hearty appearance and the cheap jewelry she always wore gave anyone who didn't know her the impression that she was no more than fifty. One day, Guru Kyi wove her hair into slender braids and oiled it with marrow until it was sleek and black. Carrying a thermos full of milk tea and some steamed bread that she'd brought from Labrang, she arrived with a face wreathed in smiles. "Hehe, hey Ralo, last night . . . hehe, a guy from that camp over there, he didn't let me sleep the whole night," she said, lowering her head somewhat bashfully.

This sudden announcement shot through Ralo's body like a bolt of lightning, and in his embarrassment he didn't know how to react. "*Ah kha*, young guys these days, no shame . . ." he said.

"You're right about that. When we were young you didn't get people going to an older woman's place like that. Really, these young people today . . ." she said, casting a furtive glance at Ralo.

Ralo recalled a similar "flirtatious glance" that he'd received from the water-fetching girl many years ago and his body felt like it had been hit by another bolt of lightning, but after a moment his present circumstances came back to him. His beloved wife seemed to appear before his eyes, and he sank back into grief.

Seeing his reaction, Guru Kyi became solemn. "Ralo, it's natural to grieve, but you've done so much for the two of them since they passed. There's no need to torment yourself like this," she said, sliding over to him. "Hey, Ralo, I never knew you were so much like a woman! You're a good, devout man, it'll be easy for you to find another wife. Don't you know that saying, 'a real man is worth nine women'?" She slid closer, but Ralo remained absolutely motionless, and she gave up. "Hey, you sit around all day in a daze. Do you know what people say about you?"

Ralo, being a man very much concerned about what others thought of him, turned in a flash to face Guru Kyi. "What are people saying about me?"

"Hurry up and drink some tea, it's getting cold." Guru Kyi dropped a lump of butter into Ralo's cup, poured the tea on top, and handed it to him. "Some people are saying that you're not a real man, and some are saying . . . pah, not even the Buddha can shut the mouths of men. People say whatever comes into their heads, what can you do . . ." she said, casting Ralo another "flirtatious glance" and lowering her head like a coquettish young woman.

Ralo was still desperate to know what others were saying about him. He sidled closer to Guru Kyi. "What else are they saying about me?"

"They . . . well, they . . . pah, I'm too embarrassed to say it."

Ralo, agitated, grabbed hold of her hand, on the verge of begging her.

"They say . . . the two of us . . . pah."

Ralo completely understood now. He released her hand. "These guys love to gossip. They're nasty people," he said, shaking his head.

"You're right about that that. They were the ones that falsely accused you and got you thrown in jail. *Eh*, it's no easy thing to get by in this world without any family."

"But where am I going to get a family from?"

"Well, the ones you had can leave you, and ones you didn't can join you."

Ralo understood the meaning of her words entirely. Although Ralo and Guru Kyi weren't related, there was an age gap between them of at least ten years, so according to the customs of the region it was considered shameful for them to exchange a single word about the business between a man and a woman. From that point on, however, they were no longer bound by this taboo. This was a small victory for Guru Kyi that day.

Twenty-Two

From that day on, when she came to see Ralo, Guru Kyi got dressed up even nicer than before. Though she was a bit old, Ralo thought, she was in good shape and she was single, and he became ensnared by desire. Ralo was usually the kind of man who was fine with any woman, and he wasn't particularly interested in that sort of thing anymore either, but whenever he thought about people saying "He's not a real man," he simply couldn't bear it. One day, after he'd eaten dinner and gotten into bed, Guru Kyi came in just as he was about to go to sleep. "*Ah tsi*, it's so early, you're going to bed already?"

"I am. Why don't you get in with me?" As these words slipped out of his mouth, Ralo's heart started pounding madly. To his surprise, Guru Kyi clasped her hands to her face, lowered her head like a young woman, then ran out the door. In the face of this reaction Ralo felt embarrassed and a bit ashamed of his rash words, but then he decided that it was a good thing that he'd at least shown her he was a "real man."

That night, the faces of his wife and son appeared less often than usual on the screen of Ralo's mind. They were replaced by an image of Guru Kyi's sleek black hair and the way she clasped her hands to her face and lowered her head. Midnight came around and he still couldn't get to sleep. He rolled over onto his stomach and propped himself up on his pillow with his elbows.

A shaft of moonlight shone through the skylight of the tent, gradually descending on Ralo's "mom." The dog was covered with a calfskin blanket, on top of which was another blanket of sheepskin. The dog was now so old that it only moved when it was time to eat or drink, and it looked like it was knocking on death's door. Some days it wouldn't eat a thing, and some days it ate anything it was given, shortly after which it would pee and poop so much Ralo could hardly keep up with cleaning it. As he looked at the dog, Ralo recalled his mother. Now that he thought about it, she had been in her forties when she married his stepfather—about the same age he was now. Ralo still remembered clearly what she'd said after he walked out on them: "If I can't find a better man than that pig, then I'm no woman."

"'A real man is worth nine women.' Tamdrin Tso [the woman whose family Ralo first married into]—that's one; yellow teeth—that's two; and my dear departed—that's three." Ralo pressed his index and middle fingers to his thumb, then paused for a moment. "And Guru Kyi makes four," he said, adding his ring finger.

The shaft of moonlight shining on the dog gradually shifted away. Just as he'd done when he was a monk at the monastery, Ralo got up late and couldn't get to sleep at night, and he was haunted by loneliness. He well knew that Guru Kyi wasn't far away and that she slept alone in her own room, but he no longer dared to act as rashly as he had when he was young, so he was left alone with his web of doubts and his flights of fancy.

With no clear goal in mind, Ralo got out of bed, put on his boots, draped his jacket over his shoulders, and walked out the door. Once he was outside his gaze fell involuntarily in the direction of Chaktar's place. After he took a piss he stood lost in thought for a long time, unsure what he should do. *What if she says no? It'll be embarrassing. And what if she tells others about it? That'll be even more embarrassing. No, no,* he thought. He turned back to his door, but he didn't go in. He turned around again and stood facing Chaktar's place for some time. Eventually, a cold shiver and the chattering of his teeth shook him from his reverie, and he went back inside.

Twenty-Three

A few days later, Guru Kyi discovered that a change had taken place in Ralo's manner. She applied a healthy helping of marrow to her hair, pocketed a cheap pack of cigarettes she'd procured in advance, grabbed a dish of sweet potato rice with butter and sugar, and went to see Ralo, her head lowered, just like a young woman setting off for her first tryst.

"This . . . your family keeps giving me . . ."

"You keep saying this 'your family, my family' stuff. Let me tell you, tomorrow you should take back your land and your livestock and let Chaktar take care of it. Hm! Who else around here looks out for you, Ralo?"

"Mm . . . I don't want to trouble your family, and those people are always giving me butter and cheese."

"*Ah tsi*, still with this 'your family, my family'! What a hard person you are to get close to." Guru Kyi stuffed the pack of cigarettes into Ralo's hands. "First they stole your wife, then they had you thrown in jail on trumped-up charges. Have you forgotten?"

"Hehe, but it wasn't Akhu Loten's family that did that."

"Hm! Who can say? I'll tell you straight up, back then hardly anyone around here said that you were innocent, and now they're pretending to care, looking after your cattle for you, but everyone knows they've got designs on your land. Mm . . . and our family's land is so small . . . never mind, forget it, forget it. If you're not bothered, there's no use in me going on about it. I . . . I really see you as one of my family, Ralo. You do what you think is best." Lowering her head just like the water-fetching girl did all those years ago, Guru Kyi flashed Ralo a "flirtatious glance" and left.

That night the image of the water-fetching girl by the bank of the Tsechu appeared once more before Ralo's eyes and refused to go away. Only after his mind, an unbridled stallion, had satisfied itself with a tireless gallop through the fields of fantasy did he finally fall asleep.

A woman carrying a water pail arrived at the bank of the Tsechu. Lowering her head, she glanced at Ralo. Sometimes she appeared to be the water-fetching girl from years before, and sometimes she appeared to be another woman. Either way, she was beautiful, and she kept on casting "flirtatious glances" at Ralo. He crossed the river to get to her, or maybe she crossed toward him, and she fell into Ralo's arms. Unfortunately, both banks of the river were lined with monks, supervising them like prison guards. In desperation, Ralo grabbed her hand and they ran to his house as fast as they could. When they got there Ralo discovered that this woman was none other than Guru Kyi. The strange thing was that her whole body had become soft and supple, like that of a young woman in the prime of her life. Ralo was convulsed with desire and he threw her down on the bed.

An unpleasant, wet sort of feeling roused Ralo from his sleep. He found his crotch soaked in a sticky fluid, and he felt depressed. Eh—*I really need to get a woman*, he said to himself.

Twenty-Four

Ralo took his "mom" and the calfskin blanket to the doorway to let the dog bask in the sun, then went back inside, washed his face in a basin of warm water, and combed his braid. Ralo wasn't much for hygiene at the best of times, and he hadn't combed his braid once in the whole year since his wife and son had passed. It had become full of tangles, and brushing it was no easy task—only after enduring a good deal of pain did he finally manage to comb it all out. About a fistful of hair, full of lice eggs, was lodged in the teeth of the comb, and several of the hairs were white. Ralo's cheerful mood slowly dissipated. *I'm really getting old. Don't they say "a real man is worth nine women"? How did I get so old so quickly?* he said to himself. As he pleated his braid he looked in the direction of Chaktar's place. *Land. Woman. Give my land, get a woman. They say that pencil-necked Chaktar's a sly fox, but he's a got a big family, and not much land. If I give my land to him, then at the very least he'll have to take care of our food and clothes, for the sake of his mother if nothing else. Anyway, I need a woman by my side, that's for sure.* After this process of thought, Ralo decided to give his land to Chaktar's family.

Ralo knew very well that the basis of a nomad's livelihood was land, not cattle. He didn't have much cattle anymore, but he had enough land for three people to use. He knew too that if he rented this land to someone else he'd have no need to worry about the necessities of life. But the misery of solitude didn't give him much room to consider all of this. In Ralo's mind, Guru Kyi and the way she lowered her head and cast him "flirtatious glances" had become indistinguishable from the water-fetching girl by the banks of the Tsechu all those years ago. He jumped up all of a sudden and made his way to Chaktar's, where he made an announcement: "From today, all of my land belongs to your family."

The large group of men who were playing chess at Chaktar's place had no idea what Ralo was talking about, and they looked at one another blankly until Chaktar rose to speak. "*Ah tsi ah tsi*, Uncle Ralo you're so kind, so generous! Friends, did you hear that? Uncle Ralo said he's giving all of his land to me. Thank you, Uncle Ralo, and I'll look after your cattle as well, don't worry!"

Chaktar's friends were so amazed they forgot about their chess. "*Ah tsi ah tsi*, this Ralo is truly a bodhisattva," said some. "A man like this is truly rare these days," said others. In the midst of this chorus of praise came a diverging opinion, offered by a slightly more astute man: "Ralo, my friend, if you give your land away, how will you get by? You should think about this." He was then followed by many others. "That's right. Land is gold, land is precious. You should think about this."

Ralo looked at Guru Kyi uncertainly, and she lowered her head and cast him a "flirtatious glance." Ralo sucked in his snot, his mind completely made up. "There's nothing to think about. I have no regrets. Ralo is a man of his word."

Twenty-Five

As soon as it was light Ralo got up, washed his face, and eagerly awaited the arrival of Guru Kyi with his breakfast (in truth, Ralo no longer had the means to make himself a decent breakfast). He began to feel that a very long time had passed, but still there was no sign of Guru Kyi, so as usual he grabbed his "mom" and went outside. When it was almost noon one of the children from Chaktar's family finally arrived with a plate of sheep sausage and gave it to Ralo. It wasn't clear if this was supposed to be breakfast or lunch, but Ralo decided that it must be breakfast. After noon passed, Ralo went back to eagerly awaiting the arrival of Guru Kyi with his lunch.

In the afternoon a fierce wind began to blow, driving Ralo and his "mom" back inside, and the sun vanished behind the western hills as he continued his eager awaiting. A neighbor came to invite Ralo over for dinner, but he declined, as he was sure that Guru Kyi would soon be bringing his dinner, and also that she'd be spending the night. That night Ralo went hungry and cigarettelless. Most of all he was tormented by loneliness. Several times he was on the verge of going to find Guru Kyi, but in the end he restrained himself.

The next day Ralo arose early again, washed his face, combed his braid, and awaited the arrival of Guru Kyi with an even greater eagerness than the day before, but once more it was one of the children from Chaktar's family that brought his breakfast. Ralo was both disappointed and angry. "Why isn't your grandmother here?" he demanded, grabbing the boy's hand.

"Grandma went to the monastery yesterday."

"What did she go to the monastery for? Oh . . . I see, I see." Ralo's face broke into a smile, something that hadn't happened for some time, and he released the boy's hand. "Yes, yes, she's gone to see about the wedding day."

"Is a wedding day a good thing?" asked the boy, looking at Ralo innocently.

"Hahaha! Yes, it's a good thing. A very good thing." Ralo smacked the boy's behind merrily, and he ran off rubbing his butt with a whimper.

As he cleaned off the thick layer of dust that had accumulated on his household possessions, Ralo's restless mind was filled with expectant thoughts of his soon-to-be life with Guru Kyi. One afternoon a few days later he finally caught sight of her, but when he got close, he discovered that that sleek, glistening black hair, which inflamed his passions and which, to put it bluntly, was primarily responsible for relieving him of his land, had been completely shaved off, leaving a bald crimson pate in its place. Ralo couldn't believe his eyes. As he examined her he realized she was wearing maroon clothes that weren't quite layman's and weren't quite nun's, and the cheap jewelry that she was never without was nowhere to be seen. All of this was a horrible testament to the fact that she had taken her lay vows.

Ralo stood like a statue, mouth agape, gawking, his snot running. "Haha," he said eventually, shaking his head slowly, not knowing whether to laugh or cry. "Guru Kyi, you old hag . . ."

"My name is Chökyi Drölma now."

"Get away from me."

"*Ah tsi.*" Chökyi Drölma feigned confusion. "Are you feeling unwell or something?" she said, approaching him, but this made Ralo even more angry. He fixed her with a cold glare, then spun around and went back into his house. The house felt even more empty and silent now than it had after his wife died. He pulled the collar of his fur jacket up over his head and lay down on the floor.

After Ralo and his "mom" passed away, someone from the camp said, "*Ah ho,* looks like he's been dead for a while. If others hear about this it'll be an embarrassment to our community." One of his neighbors said, "It's been no more than two days since he passed. Yesterday morning he came over to our place, said he wasn't feeling well and that he wanted to go see Alak Drong. He asked to borrow a hundred yuan in case he had to pay for a healing ritual. 'Isn't that pencil-necked Chaktar using your land for nothing?' I said. 'Why don't you go over there and ask him? He ought to give you a hundred yuan. If he doesn't you can come back here and I'll loan it to you,' I said. But he never came back." He continued, "He really wasn't looking well at all, and he was breathing rapidly. But to just . . . *om mani padme hum*, what a pity."

When they were sorting through Ralo's possessions they discovered that there wasn't a single thing to eat in his home. Without a word to one another, they brought over some butter and lit lamps of offering, which they kept burning for seven days and nights. After this they took all his possessions, leaving not so much as a needle and thread, and donated them to the monastery. His remaining livestock were wrested from Chaktar's possession and given to Alak Drong. "*Om mani padme hum*," someone said on the way back. "Even if he'd left a will, that's all there would have been."

4

A SHOW TO DELIGHT THE MASSES

I t was a late autumn day in 1993, if you count in human years. The Lord of Death, having just reviewed and signed his name to one last document, lifted his head, stretched his arms, and with a satisfied yawn thought, *Time for a break*. It was nearly noon.

At just that moment, however, a staff member walked in with a sheet of paper and addressed him, standing at attention:

Are you free, Your Majesty?
There is a man whose time is up
today at one o'clock.
Lozang Gyatso is his name,
the Tsezhung County Governor,
in China, on the realm of Earth.
If you could authorize this soon . . .

He handed the paper to the Lord of Death and stepped aside.

The Lord of Death, with the utmost attention as always, read the document thoroughly and even verified Lozang Gyatso's age using the calculator on his desk. He then signed his name and returned the paper to his aide.

It was one o'clock sharp when Lozang Gyatso finished lunch. He figured he would quickly go to the bathroom. But as he stood up, the room went dark and before he knew what was happening, two burly men from the Public Security Bureau were leading him away by the shoulders.

"Huh? What's this? Hey! Have you gone mad? Assuming a crow hasn't plucked out your eyes, take a good look! I'm Lozang, the county governor!" he shouted fiercely, but the two forced him on without heed.

"Hey! You two sons of bitches! I'm Lozang, the county governor! Do you realize that the head of the PSB is a friend of mine? Do you realize that Sherap—the judge—is my brother-in-law? Let me go! *Ya*. Okay—you just see if I'm not a man! I'll break your rice bowls and turn you into a couple of stray dogs!"

The two messengers laughed. "Friend, even if you were the queen of England or the president of the United States, it wouldn't do you any good. Don't make it any harder on yourself. Come on. We are going to see the Lord of Death. If you were good, you'll be happier than before. If you were bad, no one can save you. We are the Lord of Death's messengers."

Slowly, it dawned on Lozang Gyatso that these two "PSB officers" were not, in fact, of this world. Rather, they were the Lord of Death's two aides, the ones mentioned in mythology: Boarhead and Bullhead. He felt a certain terror, as if molten lead had been poured into his lower legs. He couldn't take another step. With quivering lips he asked, "What? My time is up? Oh, Three Jewels! Is life so short? Really, it can't be." He shook his head.

Bullhead replied, "What? You're sixty years old, aren't you? That's not so short, as far as human lives are concerned."

"Oh . . . I still haven't found jobs for my two sons! That's why I've been waiting to write my resignation letter, even though I'm old enough to retire. Alas. My sons aren't good students. If I go now, they'll never get jobs."

He clasped his hands and began to wail loudly, singing this strain as might a howling dog:

Gracious brother messengers,
for a moment pity me.
Give me one year and I'll find
jobs for both these sons of mine.
Let me then collect my due,
for my wife will need help too.
After these deeds, then I'll come.
Whatever you need, I'll bring you some!

He beseeched them with repeated prostrations.

"What's this?" the two messengers retorted. "Stop your nonsense!" They continued steering him ahead. He grew despondent. Feeling the urge to smoke, he slid his hand into his pocket, where lay a pack of good cigarettes. He lit one, inhaled, and offered a cigarette to each of the messengers. He lit theirs as well, with a deferential show of respect.

Slightly taken aback, the two messengers nevertheless savored their cigarettes. "Tastes good. Very good!" they said.

Lozang promptly offered the rest of the pack to Bullhead. (He sensed that of the two messengers, Bullhead probably had the higher position.) "If you think so, brothers, help yourselves to more."

He adopted the bobbing head and ingratiating smile that he had used before assuming his present position, and after some sweet and sundry talk, he proposed, "Brothers, if you like these cigarettes, I have all you could want at home. Why don't I just go back and get them?"

The two messengers considered this for a moment, but replied, "No. Forget it. Once we hit the trail leading up to the Lord of Death's place we won't be able to bring anything else, not even a needle."

"Whether we bring them or not is up to you. What are you afraid of?"

"Friend, you don't understand, There's a guard at every post on the way to the great king's place. And especially now that he has that thing that looks like a glass box, one of those many computer devices that the Lord of Death imports from your world. On its face you can clearly see—even better than in the mirror the Lord of Death used to have—every last virtue and fault of any sentient being. If we let you return, there's a good chance that the king would see it. So we'd better not."

Gyatso pleaded, tears streaming down his face. "Even if he can see a person's every action during our lifetime, he can't possibly pay that much attention once we're dead. Besides, I didn't even have time to write a will for my family, my death was so sudden. Brothers, please show me some compassion!"

At that, the two messengers looked at each other and said, "It *really* is sad. Anyway, there's no place for him to escape." They nodded assent. "Okay. We'll give you twenty minutes. Go now, but come back at once. We will wait here for you."

In a flash, Lozang Gyatso was back at home. His wife and younger son were clutching at his corpse, sobbing loudly. They couldn't see him, nor could they hear when he addressed them. He was sorely disappointed.

Meanwhile, his elder son had arrived and was calling his office manager. "My father has died. It was unexpected. We need a vehicle right away."

The manager paused for a moment and then replied that he'd made plans to go somewhere with the vice-governor and since the other cars were already in use, none was available.

Lozang Gyatso's son grew angry. "Have you no shame? Do you recall that it was my father who promoted you? Have you forgotten already?"

To which the manager merely sniffed—"Pfft!"—and slammed the receiver down.

His son continued to call their family and friends. Lozang was quite sure that if he had offered any one of them his piss while he was alive, they would have drunk it. But now, they were all searching for an excuse in order to avoid any commitment.

The elder boy tried again and again to reach his younger brother and sister, who lived elsewhere. When he finally managed to inform them that their father had died, they showed not the slightest remorse. Moreover, they reminded him, "All of us have rights to Father's money and things. You can't hoard them all yourself. We all need to meet and divide them up fairly." His daughter even added, "Father told me before he died that he was going to give that gold watch of his to my husband. Nobody else should take it." (This was, in fact, a lie.)

Taking all this in, Lozang Gyatso lost any sense of attachment to the world. He took as many of his valuables as he could carry and returned to where the two messengers were waiting. Lozang treated them with the utmost courtesy and offered a gift to the guards at every post. As a result, he was spared the usual hardships along the way and soon found himself standing before the Lord of Death.

When Lozang Gyatso glanced about and noticed that the Lord of Death was alone with no staff, he began to smile. "Heh, heh. Reverend king, how are you? Healthy, right? You may have some years on you, but you're in great shape!"

Saying this, he pulled out a bottle of quality *chang* and a pack of good cigarettes, as well as some musk, white herbal medicine, butter, and *droma* [wild miniature sweet potatoes], and placed the lot down on the desk in front of him. "Heh, heh. I had to walk that long road, so I couldn't carry any more than this. These are merely a token of my goodwill."

"Good grief! Merciful Buddha!" The Lord of Death's jaw dropped as he stared wide-eyed at the items on his desk. Lozang Gyatso thought, *Now everything will be okay! As the saying goes, "A bribe will always do the trick, even with the Lord of Death." Surely he too must lust for material things, and I doubt anyone has ever brought*

*him this many gifts. But, "One has a lot of dreams if the night is long."
I'd better leave now before I miss my chance.*

He got up to go. "Hey, reverend king, look after your health.
'However important our affairs might be, health should be our
priority.' I'd best be getting along now. Oh—is Paradise still where
it used to be?"

But as Lozang made motions to leave, the Lord of Death's eyes
flashed red as lightning and his voice roared like thunder. "Sit
down!" He pounded the desk with his fist. "You, you, you . . ." He
pressed a button on his desk, and two of his aides walked in, armed
with some modern-looking contraptions. (Lozang Gyatso had
only seen such devices in foreign films.)

"This man is really something else! Take him away for now,
and keep him under close observation." The great king dis-
missed Lozang Gyatso with the two aides and picked up a yellow phone into which he barked, "Send for some staff from
Special Investigations—immediately!"

Ministers from the Lord of Death's Special Investigations
Committee began to stream in. As soon as they had all taken their
seats, the Lord of Death made the following pronouncement:

> Gathered staff, now listen up.
> This afternoon a man from Earth
> named Lozang Gyatso walked in here.
> His crafty eyes are never still.
> His talk is sweet, the nectar spills!
>
> He brought these gifts—in fact, a bribe.
> My royal eyes have never seen this type.
> That's why I've called you here. You see,
> he's not your normal sort of guy.
>
> Good or bad, I still can't tell,
> but we should really test him well.

Such is how the case strikes me.

Tell me now what you believe.

In unison, the ministers resolved, "As the king has decreed, so be it!" Seeing the objects that Lozang Gyatso had brought, they were embarrassed for the man.

The Lord of Death rose, and his two aides led Lozang Gyatso in. "*Ya!* Our enigmatic fellow! Once upon a time, in the country of China on planet Earth, people of all nationalities were oppressed by the three mountains of imperialism, feudalism, and corrupt capitalism. They were bowed down by these, and the country was a virtual hell realm. But the great Mao Zedong studied well the theories of Marx and Lenin, and in accord with the reality of conditions in China he championed the working class, established a united front with the peasants, and utterly smashed the three mountains. Differences between rich and poor were eliminated. With no distinctions between the strong and the weak or the high and the low, the country became a virtual Western Paradise ruled by the deities of earth and sky. As we know, the Communist Party—savior of those oppressed by imperialists and otherwise weak—devotes its life to the truth, thinking only of the welfare of human beings.

"And you are not only a member of the Communist Party but also a high official. In particular, having been born in the Land of Snows, the realm of Avalokiteśvara, surely you value the laws of universal love, compassion, and justice. I imagine you must be a conscientious sort. Now, tell us. Your salary having come from the country's coffers, what bit of good did you do for the people? With the authority of the Party, what just deeds did you perform? Having been granted this golden *stupa*—a human body—what legacy did you leave for sentient beings? At the same time, please tell my Special Court today—frankly and honestly—what acts of nonvirtue you have committed."

Lozang Gyatso blushed, as he couldn't recall having accomplished anything of such value during his sixty years. They knew he had been a Party member. That wasn't good, he figured, given that the Party was atheistic. He felt fearful, but taking heart when a few religious acts he had performed came to mind, he began this ingenious song:

Listen, brothers gathered here.
Your Majesty, please lend your ear.
Though I may look materialistic,
actually, I am pure Buddhistic.
Ten years after I was born,
I said my vows, my head was shorn.
But later, liberation came
and I disrobed. What's to blame?
Seeing that I was fair and square,
they offered me the accountant's chair.
Though chances to steal were many,
I never took a single penny.
For this reason I was retained.
Join the Party! they refrained.
I thought not joining would be best,
because the Party's atheist.
Yet, when some higher-ups insisted,
into the Party I was enlisted.
They made me governor, and from the start,
I served the masses with all my heart.
Once the revolution passed,
religious policy relaxed.
Only then were our minds at ease
to foster spiritual activities.
So that all might benefit from their bounty,
I called countless lamas to our county.
To help fulfill the people's every wish,
to Lhasa I have made three trips.
As for my prostrations—they're in the millions.

My circumambulations total zillions.
Khatas, money, and much more, to temples I have offered these,
whether they were large or small, Tibetan, Mongolian, or
    Chinese.
What haven't I done for religion's sake?
But you have asked what role I played!
Given what I've just outlined,
you should rush me to the realms sublime.

"All right. *Ya*. And so it is," The Lord of Death replied. "By your
talk one would think you only did good and no bad. But you
Tibetans have a saying, 'The one who knows his faults is a buddha.' Those who can admit their shortcomings are few enough,
but those who can offer a self-criticism are even rarer. Now, let's
hear from your personal *lha* and personal *dü*, who have accompanied you since birth. The former will present evidence of the vir-
tuous acts you performed; the latter will present evidence of your
wrongdoings."

At this, Lozang Gyatso's personal *lha*—a white karma cherub—
hesitantly slid down from his right shoulder. Taking a seat on the
right labeled "Defense," he uttered meekly:

If I may have a word, dear king, and ministers of the court.
I'd like to say they're mostly true—the claims he's just put forth.
To Śākyamuni he bowed low, and offered prayers and *khatas*.
To prove his religiosity, I have supporting data.
Once the court has looked at these, I'm sure you will agree
to send him on to Paradise, perhaps immediately.
"You'll never go to Hell," they say, "if once you've been to Lhasa."
Since Lozang's been there many times, this shouldn't be a hassle.

He placed a white metal box on the Lord of Death's desk and
returned to his seat.

Next, Lozang Gyatso's personal *dü*—a small black demonic-looking figure—descended from his left shoulder. With head held high and a steady step, the *dü* took the chair on the left labeled "Prosecution," surveyed the room, and declared:

If anyone knows this man, it's me.
At birth he became an orphan and was abandoned like a pup.
But a kindhearted woman took him in and made sure he grew up.
She fed him every crumb she had and clothed him as she could.
But by the time that he'd turned ten, he dreamed of better goods.

Knowing what monastics get,
he donned monk's robes and shaved his head.
The vows of refuge scarcely uttered,
he swindled nomads for feastly suppers.
But as he approached maturity,
he made a move for his security.
He broke his vows and took a wife,
intent on enjoying a secular life.

Ousting the old woman who'd fostered him, Lozang sealed her
    fate.
Due to his cold-heartedness, she starved in the famine of '58.
At that time, with China's liberation,
the poor were held in veneration.
Because with learning he'd been anointed,
as village accountant he was appointed.
He took all the yaks and sheep he pleased,
and cheated still others for butter and cheese.

When the winds of the Cultural Revolution came,
he pointed, "This one chants *mani*—he's insane!"
Or "He slanders the Party!"—of good men this was said.

He framed the innocent and became village head.
Then to all sorts of schemes he put his name,
while to countless monasteries he set flame.
Into the rivers he threw statues and *pechas*,
treating religious paintings as he might a mattress.
He straddled a lama as he would a horse,
and mounted Dharma wheels like a yak—or worse.
He made old monks serve as beasts of burden,
and ordered the common people to serve him.
He even pissed into the mouth of Alak Drong,
seeing no difference between right and wrong.

When his tongue had nothing else to do, harsh words crashed
    like thunder.
When his hands should otherwise be still, his fists tore things
    asunder.
Some people fled their homes, others took their lives,
unable to bear his cruelty or be wrongly criticized.
As you can see, this man was mean
and weaseled his way through the Party machine.
He first assisted Pema, governor of the county,
who mistakenly promoted him, an undeserved bounty.
Suddenly, the governor found his fortunes changed;
his assistant began to criticize him like a man deranged.
In struggle sessions, Lozang Gyatso wielded strong didactics
and framed the kindly governor with rabble-rousing tactics.
The people's praise for him was thunderous,
no accolades could be too wondrous.
"Lozang Gyatso's revolutionary stance
is more stable than South Mountain."
In a single bound, Lozang leaped to stellar heights
and managed to secure what was Pema's post by rights.
Ever since then, he's been filled with arrogance

and from the masses has kept a distance.
As he tossed their proposals over his shoulder,
his official demeanor grew ever bolder.
He rode the finest horses and drove expensive cars,
and using the most premium guns, on the landscape left
    his scars.
Musk deer, stag, and beasts of prey
fell to his poaching, day after day.
While his family and friends filled the county posts,
those who spoke their minds vanished like ghosts.
Lozang liked to spread rumors and sow dissension,
setting factions against others to divert their attention.
The easy tasks he did himself and bragged of his
    accomplishments,
while those who failed at harder tasks were doled out serious
    punishments.
To intellectuals he was especially cruel.
Yet he himself gambled with thugs, as a rule.

At one point, his avarice grew more and more.
He gave to superiors what he swiped from the poor.
He was quick with the bribes when he took 'em and made 'em.
Hailing "uncles" and "aunties," their votes he would gain them.
In meetings with some folks, their palms he greased.
Others he threatened, and his rank increased.
Though he wore the Party flag, he corruptly used its forces
to embezzle all he could of the country's own resources.
Secretly, he supported Buddhism, despite the Party's oath.
So, in effect, he harbored a disloyalty to both.
He satisfied a few high lamas by cranking up the taxes.
Feigning it was "the people's wish," to others he gained access.
His thoughts, in fact, were solely focused on his reputation,
the Party and the people's needs were just an irritation.

Lozang Gyatso shirked his work and traveled where he pleased,
the costs of which necessitated public funds be seized.
With claims that it was for the country's economic good,
he set up private businesses in any town he could.
Your messengers allowed him to return to Earth unaided.
When Lozang offered cigarettes, they finally were persuaded.
Even your own gatekeepers he similarly coaxed,
offering bribes along the way at each and every post.
Great king—you saw it!—he offered you many gifts as well,
figuring he'd use the back door as a way to escape from Hell.

Doesn't this prove that he is one beyond redemption?
Lozang Gyatso's few good deeds are hardly worth a mention.
If I were to detail his every endeavor,
all of us gathered would be here forever.
Your Majesty, if you want to reach a conclusion,
you can shut the door for months of seclusion.
But when you examine every document here,
the deeds he has done will be all too clear.
Whatever he's done is recorded—I have no secrets.
I swear by my father's flesh.
If he hasn't done it—I haven't made it up.
I swear by my mother's blood.
If I've added or omitted a single thing,
I will cut my own son's throat.

With these concluding oaths, he stacked upon the Lord of Death's desk eighteen black metal boxes with all the records of wrongdoings that Lozang had committed during his life. The pile cast a shadow on the Lord of Death's massive figure, like the shadow of the sun's eclipse.

Two of the king's court attendants took the boxes of documents from the desk, and the Lord of Death became visible again. With a white handkerchief, he wiped beads of sweat as large as peas from his face. "Oh my, Merciful Buddha!" He looked agitated and took a couple of sips of coffee. Feeling a bit calmer, he said, "*Ya*. You're a smooth talker. Is what the public prosecutor claimed just now true? According to section 3, chapter 8 of the Lord of Death's Litigation Code, if you, the defendant, have anything to say for yourself, you may do so. But tell the truth!"

However, Lozang Gyatso said nothing. Only when one of the judges nudged him and Lozang Gyatso toppled out of his chair did they realize he had fainted. The Lord of Death's doctor arrived and placed a pill into the defendant's mouth. Lozang Gyatso's body convulsed, and he eventually revived. The trial continued.

The Lord of Death repeated his words for a second time, but Lozang Gyatso did not reply. He prompted him once more. "Does the defendant have anything to say?"

The personal *lha* raised his hand to speak. "It is true—as the prosecutor has just stated—that during the Cultural Revolution, our man Lozang Gyatso tortured lamas and monks, accused the innocent, and burned down monasteries. However, because of historical forces at that time, most of the population was engaged in such activities. Countless numbers of people even struggled against their own parents, and so forth. Since history is also at fault, it is not fair to place the blame entirely on my client.

"Furthermore, as for my client taking government money, accepting bribes, and so forth, during these last few years—that is the fault of the current bad social climate. It is not just my client. Many people are under bad influences, and there are even such men in the Lord of Death's own realm. This is a social condition, not something for which my client alone can be held responsible.

"Finally, my client performed many good acts. In any case, he has committed no serious crimes, and the wrongdoings we mentioned earlier were rather minor."

As soon as Lozang Gyatso's *lha* had finished speaking, his personal *dü* raised his hand to talk. "The defendant has made the following claim: 'Though I may look materialistic, actually I am pure Buddhistic.' As everyone knows, according to the Lord of Death's constitution, whether one is a Buddhist or not, whether one is a Party member or not, does not matter. What is important is one's own faith and that one holds one's tenets purely. As a member of the Party, which adheres to no religion of any sort, the defendant, Lozang Gyatso, in fact, opposed the Party by secretly engaging in religious activity. This clearly demonstrates that he is a criminal who cannot be trusted. And he said it wasn't his fault that he had to give up his robes after his homeland was liberated. That was a lie. Just look at human history! In 1948 he broke his vows and gave up his robes. But the defendant's homeland was only liberated in 1950.

"The defendant also lied when he said that he fell under the Party's control gradually. He actively and ambitiously sought out positions and wrote seven letters for the purpose of joining the Party." After presenting the Lord of Death with several documents, the *dü* continued. "Furthermore, he said that he thought the Party wasn't good because they were atheist and therefore he didn't want to stay in it. This expresses his resistance to the Party.

"Moreover, one cannot blame history and society, as the defense has just claimed in explaining this man's wheelings and dealings during the Cultural Revolution. As everyone knows, if a person has good principles and stands up for them, even when such social transformations occur, he knows the difference between right and wrong and would quite possibly even give up his life for the truth without regret. No-brains like this man, who are indifferent to the laws of karma, will lean whichever way the wind blows, like grass on a wall.

"It is true the defendant made offerings to many monasteries, invited many lamas to receive empowerments, and went to Lhasa to prostrate before Jowo Rinpoché. But it is a sad fact that all of the money he used was from exploiting the toiling masses' flesh and blood. Not only were these not the fruits of his own labor, but he also pocketed much of the money, and the amount the monasteries received was but a sliver of the total he collected."

When it was apparent that Lozang Gyatso could again say nothing, or had nothing to say, the little *lha* seized his last chance. Hanging on by a horsetail, he asserted: "With regard to my client offering cigarettes to the Lord of Death's messengers and carrying these gifts with him, may I remind you of the saying: 'There is no seller without a buyer.' Likewise, no one can offer a bribe without somebody to accept it. Given that the Lord of Death's own messengers are at fault in this matter, how can my client alone be blamed?"

It was as if these words opened the door of the Lord of Death's mind. "Hmm . . . how *was* it that you carried these things here?"

Lozang Gyatso reflected, *Since they know everything anyway, there's no use holding back now.* He then related the entire story about how he had given cigarettes to Boarhead and Bullhead, how the two had sent him back, how he had offered the things he brought as bribes to each of the gatekeepers, and how he consequently didn't have to face any great difficulties along the way.

Lozang Gyatso was dumbfounded, however, when his *dü* interjected with the following: "Everyone should think about this. If a person were good, it would be impossible for him to sell out on someone to whom he owed so much, even if he were on his deathbed. Yet this cheater, without a second thought, even sold out on the two kind messengers who let him go back because of their compassion for him. From this, one can clearly see that the defendant is an inferior sort who betrays those who have treated him kindly."

In any case, the Lord of Death immediately summoned Boarhead and Bullhead before the court and questioned them. He then ordered a number of the gatekeepers to set aside their work and write statements regarding their actions.

Then, all who were gathered in the Lord of Death's Special Investigations Court examined the small white cardboard boxes with their two videocassettes on which were recorded the merits Lozang Gyatso had accumulated in his life. Next, they turned to the seventy small black cardboard boxes whose contents documented his demerits. After every last videocassette had been examined, the Lord of Death sighed. "Okay. There is no need for further discussion regarding your merits and demerits. All can be clearly seen here. Now, in keeping with the Lord of Death's Litigation Code, the public prosecutor, the defending attorney, and the defendant himself all have the right to make a final statement. So if you have anything to say, speak now!"

The personal *lha* spoke first:

Ministers and, above all, the Lord of Death, please hear me out.
It is true that my client Lozang has committed many crimes.
However, as I said before, he is a product of the times.
In a rotten social climate, one might as well be cursed.
Many people there on Earth behave like him and worse.
If you send this man to Hell, you'll have to send the rest.
The eighteen realms will overflow, and that would be a mess.
So think about the future. What are you going to do?
Where will you put the others who've committed these
    crimes too?

The Lord of Death removed his glasses and furrowed his brow. He sat for a while, then let out a long breath and shook his head from side to side. "That's true. This is really an issue." And he continued pondering for some time.

Alak Drong had first received word of Lozang Gyatso's death when he was offered a horse along with the request to offer prayers for the deceased. He spontaneously responded, "*Ah ho!* What a shame." *Why did he have to die just now?* he wondered. Feeling a great deal of remorse, he tugged on his lower cheek. With his omniscient eyes, he had a look into the Lord of Death's realm and saw that they were still deciding how to punish Lozang Gyatso. He immediately shed his Chinese clothes and put on his monk's robes. Then he hopped into his car and drove off, reciting mantras. After some time, he arrived at the border of the Lord of Death's realm.

The border guard was extremely respectful as he blocked Alak Drong's path and asked the lama where he had come from, where he was going, the purpose of his travel, and to please produce his passport. Alak Drong leaned his cheek on his left hand, and while revving the gas pedal with his right foot, sang this short heroic song:

Aro, Border Guard for the Lord of Death!
With your ears of a pig and eyes of a pup,
turn them here and listen up.
This is a car, yet it flies through the sky,
and all because the driver is I.
In my first life, I was in the Buddha's throng.
Now they call me Alak Drong.
At Tsezhung Monastery, I am a lama,
a devout protector of the Buddha Dharma.
Today, for the sake of every sentient being,
I have come to find the One All-Seeing.
I must speak to him without delay.
So do not dally. Clear the way!

The border guard didn't understand Alak Drong's song clearly, but he decided that the man inside this car that could fly through the sky was a living being, and certainly no ordinary one. This set him at ease, and he was happy to reverentially step aside and say, "Have a good journey."

Alak Drong pulled up to the door of the Lord of Death's court, applying the brake with a screech. After grabbing a *khata* and a few blocks of tea previously offered him by a faithful Buddhist, he moved to enter the building. Through the clear glass walls, however, he could see that the Lord of Death and the judiciary ministers were seated inside the courtroom, each absorbed in thought. Alak Drong paused. *I need to meet with the Lord of Death alone. It's not good to talk about such matters in front of a lot of people.* But then, reconsidering, he thought: *Once the Lord of Death makes a decision and stamps it with his seal, it will all be over, won't it?* He decided to proceed inside. *At the same time, I am a lama, and there is little precedent for a person of my stature to make such an unfounded request amid a group of so many people.* As opportunity would have it, while Alak Drong was wondering what he should do, the time came for the afternoon recess and the ministers emerged from the courtroom and headed home.

Alak Drong got back into his car and slowly followed the Lord of Death. When they reached the king's quarters, Alak Drong lowered his monk's shawl out of respect and held out the aromatic tea packages with the unsullied *khata*, while singing this verse to the melody of chanted *mani*:

Respected king, Lord of Death,
in the fine glass house with no wooden beams,
in keeping with the customs of the Land of Snows,
please grant me consideration in accepting this *khata*,
an unsullied silk offering scarf.
I will tell you in detail my purpose for coming.
They call me Alak Drong.
I'm a lama from Tsezhung Monastery.
There are many fine things that I could offer.

Since we are already acquaintances, however,

I have come bringing only this splendid *khata* and tea.

We meet again through the fortune of good circumstances!

Though I am practically empty-handed with this simple tea,

recall that tea is known by all to sustain life.

But I will set aside the usual chatter and

slowly tell you all in a manner as clear as the full moon:

I am here about Lozang Gyatso, an official

who was a gentleman in name only,

a scoundrel who very much liked to smoke.

Until recently, he was alive and in good health,

and only just passed away.

Though it was time for him to die,

given that he had lived to a ripe age,

Please recall that in these last couple of years

he became a fervent believer in Buddhism

and fostered it with concern, as a father might a son.

He restored countless monasteries,

and converted many in his land to Buddhism.

He served the people as might a cow.

He invited lamas with motherlike compassion and

the characteristic sign of their hair growing in the reverse

    direction.

He fulfilled the wishes of sentient beings.

He collected merit by visiting Mount Tsari in Ü-Tsang

and established many religious reliquaries for *tsakali* images.

He established fine and splendid stupas, and

thought not about his nieces and nephews, but of the Dharma.

Though he burned valuable teachings during the Cultural

    Revolution,

if one thinks carefully about it now during this period of

    regret-lined

happiness, many beings behaved like cunning foxes then,

wearing their green military hats and red armbands.

Suppression of the Yellow Hat doctrine was the fault of the
    times.

Nowadays everyone is ambitious;

those who know their proper share are rare.

Compared to the truly evil officials, brother Lozang isn't bad.

In these heartless times, if one doesn't rely down there

on the officials who hold power,

the teachings of the Buddha that have gone numb

are hard to protect.

It's like keeping a wolf out of the pasture.

Please, out of your great compassion,

give Lozang Gyatso back his life, his flesh and blood

for the benefit of all sentient beings everywhere,

so that they may quickly realize the teachings of the Buddha.

Send him back to Earth so that he might work a bit for beings
    there.

It is very difficult to ask you this.

Please don't laugh, Compassionate One,

Please don't say "No" to this poor old lama.

Respected king, please give this your consideration.[1]

Saying this, he prostrated, touching his forehead to the ground.
At which the Lord of Death said, "Don't do that. Please get up
now, sit on a chair, and listen to my song":

My dear lama—

Your words were spoken most eloquently.

---

1. Alak Drong's long verse was originally written using a version of
"alphabet poetry" (*ka rtsom*), in which the first two lines each start with A,
the next two lines with B, and so forth. The translator has omitted this
convention in order to retain the meaning of the verse.

Now I have something to say of my own.
Except for one Gesar Norbu Dradül,
you're the finest man to approach my throne.

I never knew much about life on Earth,
but if the situation is really as you claim,
on the one hand it has some good points,
but it mostly sounds a shame.

In any case, I won't send your man to Hell,
though Lozang Gyatso's life was long.
He accumulated a lot of demerits,
but I am moved by your faith and song.

As a king who turns the Wheel of Dharma,
I'm not in the habit of sending them back.
We don't let lice and nits live long.
Such is the world. But you know that.

My words here are not necessary,
because you are a lama.
But, for this reason, please return
and protect the Buddha Dharma.

Upon hearing these words Alak Drong was deeply ashamed,
but he recalled the saying, "It's important not to hold on to the
tail of a tiger, but if you do, then don't let go." Figuring there was
nothing else he could do, he began prostrating. Concerned that it
would hurt the merit of one in monastic robes to prostrate so
much, the great king urged him, "Don't do that. Get up! Get up!"
However, Alak Drong persisted. "No. I am just taking orders.
I am simply a messenger arrow released by the man's family to look
after his welfare, not to mention my accepting that horse. I can't

go back without fulfilling my task. So please, great king, if you can't give Lozang Gyatso eternity, at least give him a little more time. If you can grant this, I swear on the Three Jewels that I will stop prostrating before you here today." He bore on as stubbornly as a yak.

The Lord of Death grew even more perturbed. "*Ah tsi!*" he said, starting to pace back and forth. "This one is really something else."

When it really looked as if the lama was not about to rise, the great king tried a last resort: "Okay. First, get up, and then the two of us can talk."

Like a peacock excited by the sound of thunder, Alak Drong immediately replied: "Yes, sir. Thank you, great king."

The Lord of Death relaxed upon hearing these words. He wondered at this person who—like a true bodhisattva—could offer such unselfish assistance to a man who had previously made the lama drink his piss. He was especially happy to accommodate this lama who, unlike others, still showed interest in the consciousness of the deceased, even after he'd received the horse offering. *It wouldn't be so bad*, he thought, *if I were to temporarily place Lozang Gyatso in this fellow's stead so that he could clear himself of the karma he has collected from his wrongdoings. Is it not recorded in the legal code of the Lord of Death?* "*The verdicts made here are so that a good man might later come.*"

"*Ya,* old monk. There is a Chinese saying: 'Though you might not notice a monk on his own account, because of his lama you do.' And there is a Tibetan saying: 'Though you wouldn't buy the horse for its looks, if the saddle is good you should.' Like these, given that it is you who have come here, I really have no option. I permit you to temporarily take Lozang Gyatso back with you so that he might redeem himself. However . . ."

Before the Lord of Death had finished speaking, Alak Drong got up, thinking he had better head back: "If the night is long, one has many dreams."

"Yes, sir. Yes, sir," he said, making moves to leave. But the Lord of Death stopped him: "*However*, you must take back these gifts."

When the king handed back the items that he'd been offered, Alak Drong protested, "No. No. You mustn't. If you do that, I will end up in the otherworld. You mustn't think like that." Again, he got up and tenaciously prostrated before the great king, who ordered: "If you don't take these back, I will not release Lozang Gyatso to you!" At which point, the lama relented and took the gifts back.

As soon as Alak Drong got back to Earth, he went straight to Lozang Gyatso's house and with great conceit announced: "You needn't suffer anymore! Take a look at this!" He then breathed on the corpse of Lozang Gyatso, who regained consciousness. Though Alak Drong tried to restrain him, Lozang Gyatso grabbed at anything and gulped it down as if within him had grown an insatiable hunger and thirst. The memory of all that had happened in the Lord of Death's realm evaporated like a rainbow. However, sometime after the initial lapse of memory, he began to realize what had happened. And when his family told him about how Alak Drong had breathed on him, how Lozang Gyatso had revived, and so forth, he prostrated again and again to Alak Drong, beseeching: "Root Lama to whom I am so grateful, the one who has given me life again! Just tell me! Whatever you need in this world—the sun, the moon, the stars—anything at all, be frank. If I can't get it for you, then I, Lozang Gyatso, am a dog!"

Alak Drong thought, *Since this is a man who easily forgets those to whom he is indebted, it would be best to have him attend to some matters now.* Being a clever man, however, Alak Drong merely replied, "County Governor Lozang Gyatso, sir, if you were to support the Buddha Dharma with all your heart forevermore, then my giving you life again would all be worth it. You don't need to do anything for me."

After a considerable length of time spent discussing various and sundry things, it seemed that Alak Drong suddenly remembered something. "Oh! That's right. Though there isn't any question that my nephew is the reincarnation of Alak Yak, in these degenerate times, so many people are wont to dispute a lama's succession. You should be careful about this business," he warned.

"Don't you worry!" Lozang reassured him. "If your nephew doesn't get approved, then I'm an old dog!" And the recognition of Alak Drong's nephew as the reincarnation of Alak Yak was thereupon secured.

Some days later, it occurred to the Lord of Death to muse, "I wonder if there's any information regarding Lozang Gyatso's acts of atonement." He looked down toward Earth. *Ah kha!* As if bitten by a rabid dog and gone mad, Lozang Gyatso had fired those who refused to help when he was dead, caused innocent others to be imprisoned, pulled into the workplace his own sons and even his grandsons who had not yet finished primary school, promoted or given positions to all of his relatives, and finally appointed his illiterate wife, who couldn't spell her own name, as director of the Cultural Bureau. These acts, at which the official's superiors had chuckled and his subordinates had wept, enraged the great king, who thereupon reached down and, grabbing Lozang Gyatso by the scruff of his neck, threw him into the cauldron of Hell, at which the masses applauded ecstatically.

Translated by Lauran Hartley

5

ONE *MANI*

ONE

Just as the bedridden Gendün Dargyé was calmly reciting his ninety-nine million nine hundred ninety-nine thousand nine hundred and ninety-ninth *mani* he was struck by a sudden, intense pain, and without even having a moment to realize it, he was taken into the next life. At around the same time, Gendün Dargyé's sole sworn brother, Tsering Samdrup, had the sensation that he wasn't long for this world, and, folding his hands over his heart, murmured, "May the six classes of sentient beings that have been our mothers attain liberation and reach the level of omniscience. I pray that humanity may have equality, freedom, and peace. *Om mani padme hum*," immediately after which he drifted off as if into a peaceful sleep and set out on the narrow path to the netherworld.

Among the teeming throng of tens of thousands of transiting souls, Gendün Dargyé and Tsering Samdrup were reunited.

"Haha! It's really true what they say—even in the afterlife sworn brothers will be brought together." Tsering Samdrup, grinning broadly and looking completely carefree, approached Gendün Dargyé and grasped his hand, just like he used to when they were still in the land of the living. But Gendün Dargyé simply stood there expressionless, his face drained of all color, shaking his head.

"What's the matter, my brother?" asked Tsering Samdrup as he put his arm around Gendün Dargyé and helped him to the side of the road.

Gendün Dargyé continued to shake his head sorrowfully. "A shame . . . what a shame, I . . . I must be cursed," he said finally, now on the verge of tears.

"*Ah ho*, my brother, what on earth has happened to you?"

"Don't they say that if you recite one hundred million *manis* you're sure to go to the Blissful Realm?"

"Yeah, I think that's what they say. Why?"

"*Eh*," he said, sighing, "do you know how many *manis* I did?"

"You're always reciting your *manis*, aren't you? You've done a lot by now, I'd guess, maybe even a hundred million. You should be happy!"

"*Eh*," he said, sighing again, "let me tell you: I recited ninety-nine million nine hundred ninety-nine thousand nine hundred and ninety-nine *manis*—I was short of a hundred million by just one. You tell me, do I have bad karma or what?"

"Hahahaha! So that's what you're worried about?"

"Yes! It's no laughing matter."

"In that case, you can set your mind at ease."

"?"

"Well, as you know, I pretty much wasted my life away goofing around. I was never able to save up any money, and I never did any chanting or spiritual practices either. But, just before I died, I recited one *mani*. I'll give you that *mani*."

"Wh . . . what? Did I hear that right? Say that one more time."

"I'm giving you my only *mani*."

"You . . . you . . . you've always been a kidder, haven't you? It's not right for you to make fun of me over such an important thing."

"*Ah ya*, you're so . . . It's just one *mani*. We're sworn brothers—
what's one *mani*?"

"Brother, my wonderful brother!" Gendün Dargyé, deeply
moved, tears welling in his eyes, embraced Tsering Samdrup. "You
know that when I was still in the human world you were my only
sworn brother—no others—and it was absolutely the right choice.
This must be my good karma."

"That it must. Ah . . . who knows if we two brothers will get
another chance to meet after this. Why don't we recount some of
our stories, remember the happy times together?"

"Yes, that'd be nice, but . . . I'm still not feeling completely com-
fortable about this. What'll we do if the Lord of Death says your
mani can't be transferred to my account? So . . . so wouldn't it be
best if we went to see the Lord of Death now and explained the
situation to him?"

"Oh, yes—let's do that. The *bardo* path isn't a very nice place to
be, either."

Truly, it was a murky, ashen-colored place, a place that was neither dark nor light. Apart from the countless masses of mistlike
dead, there wasn't a sentient being or living thing to be seen. It
was a realm that evoked feelings of terror and loathing at the same
time.

The two of them rejoined the ranks of the tens of thousands of
departed souls. Like a mother guiding her naughty child, Gendün Dargyé led Tsering Samdrup through the wavelike crowds,
never letting go of his hand even for a second.

TWO

The Lord of Death's offices were located in a newly built Western-
style high-rise next to the former law courts. The building was
divided into five large departments. Each employee had a computer

in front of them, and each computer formed part of an online network with access to a database that exhaustively recorded and calculated all the virtues and vices and good and evil thoughts of all the departed souls from the five continents of the earth. It is said that on average each employee could process the virtues and vices and good and evil thoughts of one departed soul and send them to the appropriate destination—be that the Blissful Western Realm or the worlds of the Six Beings—within thirty seconds. Despite this, there were still tens of thousands of departed souls arranged into numerous lines, all waiting to register in a huge hall bigger than a football field.

On the walls of the great hall were a number of large color screens. Some were showing video footage of the achievements of political and religious leaders who had made contributions to the freedom of humankind; of the accomplishments of scientists, thinkers, artists, charity workers, environmental activists, animal rights activists, and others who had worked toward the spiritual and material well-being of humankind; and of how, after death, they were encircled by beautiful deities and escorted to Shambhala, or back to a developed democratic country where they could continue to achieve great things. The other screens were showing video footage of the crimes of dictators, deployers of nuclear weapons, destroyers of the environment, corrupt officials, drug dealers, and others who had incited wars or trampled on the rights of races, nations, and individual human beings, and of how, after death, they were taken to the hell realms, where they suffered unspeakable torments.

Gendün Dargyé finally managed to guide Tsering Samdrup to the registration desk, where he gave a detailed account of his situation. The case was perhaps a bit too complicated for the employee on duty—at least, he said that it was beyond his authority to decide and he would have to pass it up to his superiors, and he informed them that he had transferred the file containing their vices and virtues and good and evil thoughts to the Lord of Death's computer. Much to their surprise, Bullhead and Boarhead, the Lord of Death's messengers, arrived on the spot to bring Gendün Dargyé and Tsering Samdrup directly before the Great Lord himself.

"Is this true?" asked the Lord of Death, deeply moved and completely dumbfounded, as he partly arose off the throne from which he had never arisen before, then sat himself down again.

Gendün Dargyé and Tsering Samdrup, rather unsure of what was going on, looked at each other for a moment, then turned back to face the Lord of Death.

The Lord of Death took a look at his computer screen. "So, Tsering Samdrup wishes to donate the only *mani* that he recited in his entire life to Gendün Dargyé, is that right?"

Tsering Samdrup answered him without giving it a second thought: "Yes, that's correct."

The Lord of Death said, "Have you heard the Tibetan proverb 'As rare as a *mani* in the next life?'"

"Of course I have."

"Then you understand the meaning of this saying?"

"Well, I think it means something incredibly valuable, something very hard to come by."

"And yet you still consent to bequeath your sole *mani* to another, without hesitation?"

"Of course. Gendün Dargyé and I are sworn brothers. If I weren't even willing to give up a single *mani*, wouldn't 'sworn brothers' be an empty title?"

"How marvelous! You are a man of true virtue!" The Lord of Death leaped suddenly from his seat and rushed over to shake Tsering Samdrup's hand, then led him insistently to his throne, upon which he seated him. Picking up the phone, he announced, "A man of true virtue has arrived. Escort him immediately to the Blissful Realm—no, prepare a banquet—after we have dined I shall accompany him myself!"

Tsering Samdrup, feeling very uncomfortable now, rose to his feet. "Great King, this is too . . ." he began, but the Lord of Death placed a hand on his shoulder and forced him back into the chair. "*Eh.* The people of Earth are becoming more self-centered with each passing day—just look at Gendün Dargyé. Gendün Dargyé, let me ask you: you have all these *manis*, and yet not only do you not give any to your sworn brother, you have no qualms about taking his sole *mani* for yourself, is that so?"

"That's . . . that's . . ." said Gendün Dargyé in a feeble voice, apart from which he was unable to muster any other response.

"Have you no shame?" boomed the Lord of Death as he beat his fist on the table.

Gendün Dargyé lowered his head.

The Lord of Death paced back and forth. "I truly have no idea whether or not you held in your heart the sentient beings that have been your mothers as you were chanting all those *manis*. Therefore, I also have no idea whither I should send you."

"Great King, Great King, it seems that I have harmed my sworn brother . . ." said Tsering Samdrup in a fluster, but the Lord of Death cut him off. "No no no. This has nothing to do with you. All his vices and virtues and his good and evil thoughts are recorded in his file. Whither he should be sent is also clearly stipulated in the Lord of Death's legal code. I am simply reminding him. To be truthful, Gendün Dargyé has committed no great sin, bar his excessive selfishness. In any case, he still recited all those *manis*, so he shan't be sent to the hell realms," he said, breaking into a smile.

"Oh, that's good, that's good."

"Now let us dine!"

"Ah . . . Great King, I have a request . . ."

"By all means."

"May I be permitted to have this last meal with my sworn brother?"

"How marvelous! Pure friendship, friendship of purity! Once again you have touched this old man's heart. Come, come, please come!"

The Lord of Death threw his arms around the shoulders of the two sworn brothers, and together they marched across the thick green carpet toward the banquet hall.

6

MAHJONG

According to a Japanese legend, the evil of tobacco was first brought into the human world by a demon. I have nothing against the Japanese, but there's never been such a thing as a demon in this world and there never will be, so that story is nothing but baseless nonsense. However, it is a fact that the game—or gambling tool—known as mahjong was first brought to Tsezhung by a cadre who had been fired from his government job. When he first arrived in Tsezhung he wasn't even wearing a presentable pair of trousers, but he was carrying a brand-new mahjong set consisting of green and white plastic tiles. According to him, they were made of turquoise and ivory. The people of Tsezhung, naïve as someone who "knows no person but their mother and knows no earth but the hearth," bought this completely. "This thing must be worth be a whole lot of yaks and sheep then?" said one of the wealthier men.

"How many yaks is a turquoise necklace worth? How many rams are ivory prayer beads worth?" the man retorted haughtily.

"Come on, tell me honestly. How many yaks and sheep do you want for it?" insisted the wealthy man.

"Alas, I don't want to sell it."

The man wasn't a nomad or a soldier, and he certainly wasn't a cadre anymore, yet the people of Tsezhung still called him "cadre" with a tone of reverence. The "cadre" gathered together a few unemployed young men like himself and showed them how to play, occasionally even handing each of them a cigarette, much to the delight of the nomads, who generally led uneventful lives. They spent day and night with him, and before long they had picked up the game of mahjong. Next, the "cadre" taught them how to bet, and the nomads were even more delighted. The "cadre" laid down a cash stake, then went about tirelessly relieving the nomads of their money, and he even had the pipes out of their pockets and the coats off their backs. The "cadre" could never forget how the real cadres had so heartlessly driven him out the door, butt naked, so he had no qualms whatsoever about leaving the nomads butt naked too. He even went one step further. "If there's a real man here, put up your wife. Who's got the guts to wager?" he goaded them.

Though no one dared to put up his wife, they started to bet their yaks and their sheep, leaving a few of them completely dispossessed of their livestock. Some begged him helplessly and some cajoled him desperately, but the "cadre" simply snorted with derision. "Hmph! You're free not to bet, but you're not free to shirk your debt. It's written in the laws of the nation—don't you know how many years in jail you get for not paying your debts?"

The nomads of Tsezhung didn't know a thing about the law, but they knew it was something to be feared, so they had no choice but to wager their wives. The more sensible elders then became flustered and, hoping that there might be a ritual with the power to destroy this demon called mahjong, went to see Alak Drong. Upon seeing him, however, they ended up even more flustered, and left his place looking at one another, completely unsure what to do. This was because Alak Drong, his consort, and his entourage had been deeply immersed in their own game of mahjong, and though they had approached and knelt before him, remaining that way for some time, he hadn't noticed them at all.

"If Rinpoché is playing too, how could we possibly have called it a demon?"

"We have committed great sins!"

"Unspeakable, unspeakable sins!"

When, in accordance with the instructions of the higher authorities, we went to investigate why several of Tsezhung's households had become suddenly impoverished, we found the place covered in low, square-shaped earthen mounds that resembled incense altars. These, as it turned out, were the places the shepherds conducted their mahjong games, or gambling sessions. By then, however, the "cadre" who had first popularized mahjong in Tsezhung had already made off with all its wealth and gone back to the county seat, where he was caught by the police while gambling with the real cadres. It is said that not long after the first time the "cadre" made off to the county seat with all of Tsezhung's wealth he came back again, plagued by hunger and cold and looking half dead, nothing on his body but a loincloth made from a tattered old towel. Yet, in his hands, he carried five "turquoise and ivory" mahjong sets, and instantly became rich once again.

When we confiscated all of the mahjong sets in Tsezhung an old man seized my leg, wailing. "Please, sirs! I traded a hundred rams for this; now I don't own a thing of value but this mahjong set. Have pity on me, I beg you!" The sight of him was enough to make you feel sympathy, sadness, and anger all at once.

7

THE STORY OF THE MOON

"**G**randpa, tell us a story!" the last group of children on earth—who didn't wear even a scrap of bark, much less animal skin—begged the old man pitifully.

This world, where the mountains and plains were bereft of flowers and no water flowed in the riverbeds, was silent and sorrowful. The lives of the children, who had no lessons to go to and no games to play, were even more dull and barren. And so, all day long they surrounded the elders and pleaded for stories.

"Hmm, all right, all right."

"Thank you, Grandpa! Thank you . . ." The overjoyed children clapped their little hands.

"Once upon a time, there was a princess who was as beautiful as the moon on the fifteenth . . ."

"Grandpa, what's a moon?"

"The moon? Oh, well, a long time ago the moon was the closest heavenly body to our earth. Every thirty days it would rise in the sky at dusk, looking just like the curved eyebrow of a pretty girl. With each passing day it would grow rounder and clearer, and after about ten days it was all white and round—absolutely beautiful. For that reason, the ancients always compared a pretty girl to the moon."

"Well, why isn't it here anymore?"

The old man sighed. "Then let me tell you the story of the moon. In the time of my grandfather, we human beings had very advanced science and technology, and the achievements of these skills were many. But some scientists thought that the natural environment of the earth was bad, and the reason for global climate change was that the orbit of the earth was slightly askew. If, when the moon passed over Antarctica, they could blow it up with explosives, a large amount of lunar soil would fall into the Pacific Ocean, and then the orbit of the earth would be corrected.

"Back then, human beings had many nuclear weapons with the power to destroy the earth ten times over, and the moon was only a quarter the size of the earth, so needless to say they would have had no problem blowing it up.

"The scientists ignored people's protests. With all their technology—spaceships, space stations, lasers, nuclear facilities, radio telescopes, supercomputers, robots—and with the help of all the brightest and best minds in science, they blew the beautiful moon to smithereens.

"Upon witnessing this fearsome spectacle, the peoples of other planets—whose science was very very advanced—thought, *So badly have the terrestrials defiled the mother Earth on which they depend that living beings there can hardly breathe anymore, and now they've even stretched their claws into space and destroyed the most beautiful of the heavenly bodies in the solar system. How terrible! We can't let them carry on like this, no matter what.* And so they destroyed all civilization on earth. Not only was all of humankind cast back once more into a primitive state, but waves of natural disasters and epidemics on an even greater scale than in the past wiped out hundreds of millions of people, leaving us in the situation you see today."

"Grandpa, you just made that up! It's not a true story. Go back to the story of the princess."

The children didn't like the story of the moon because they'd never heard of things like "science and technology," "nuclear weapons," and "space stations," and they had no idea what those words meant.

The old man had no choice but to tell them a story from the age of civilization, about a princess who died of a drug overdose and destroyed her whole family. . . .

8

A FORMULA

The first thought that entered his mind when he woke up was that they had to move camp today. He had come up with this plan the night before while curled up in bed with his wife. Earlier in the evening it had started drizzling, and he'd thought that if they didn't move this worn-out tent to high ground now, they'd run the risk of getting flooded.

As he went out for a piss—shoeless, sheepskin coat draped over his shoulders, chanting prayers as he went—the rays of the morning sun were beginning to show over the tip of the mountain in the east. The sound of birds singing was everywhere, their voices blending together into one great melody. The globeflowers blooming on each bank of the nearby river had multiplied since the day before, and a newborn calf was gamboling playfully around their tent. All of this gave him a feeling of contentment that was hard to put into words. But they needed to move camp today—he had no time to savor this good mood.

"Hurry up and get breakfast made, we've got to move camp today!" he announced, doing up his belt.

"*Ah tsi!*" his wife exclaimed. "We only moved here yesterday!"

"But there's a risk we'll get flooded down here in the valley. Besides, it's nice to be on high ground in the summer."

His wife, who always did just what her husband said, buttoned her lip. After finishing their breakfast, they started to gather up their things. He brought the three old yaks over and fitted their saddles. They pulled up the pegs and put them inside the tent, and after folding up the tent and binding it with ropes they loaded it onto the left side of one of the pack animals. He shouldered the leather-covered wooden chest containing all the family possessions that had been passed down to them from their grandparents or great-grandparents and strapped it to the animal's right side. Seeing that the other side now seemed a bit light, he packed the tent poles on top to balance it out. He then heaped some grain, butter, cheese, clothes, and other odds and ends onto another of the yaks. On one side of the oldest and most docile yak he packed the pans and buckets, and on the other he hung the basket they used for collecting dung and lined it with a fur rug, into which he placed their butt-naked, snot-nosed little son, whose face hadn't been washed since the day he was born. Finally, half bending and half squatting, he carefully lifted the altar onto his back and made one last sweep of the camp. Though they hadn't left anything behind except the earthen stove—which always has to be abandoned when you move camp—he couldn't shake the feeling that they'd forgotten something. He looked around, furrowing his brow, and finally discovered that the dog was still there, tied to its post.

"Ah—that's it." Laying down the altar, he yanked at the thick stake in the ground, eventually pulling it out and freeing the dog. Kneeling down again, he hoisted the altar onto his back.

His wife untied their dairy cows, coiled up the rope, and threw it over her shoulder, and they were all ready to go. By then the sun was already high in the sky, so without further delay they set off, herding the livestock and pack animals before them.

As they were pitching the tent at their new camp his wife accidentally caught the edge of her coat on the altar, dragging it to the ground and causing the bronze statue of the Buddha inside to come tumbling out. For an instant she stood, stunned, then began to recite in a flustered panic: "*Vajrasattva, Vajrasattva . . .*"

For a moment he too was aghast. Recovering himself, he dashed over and slapped his wife across the face, hard.

"*Vajrasattva, Vajrasattva . . .*" His wife had long since become accustomed to her husband's brutality. Paying no attention to the slap, she righted the altar and put the statue back inside.

He put his feet up and ate his lunch (which, like breakfast, consisted of *tsampa*), and looking out from the flap of the tent he saw white clouds gathering over the mountain peak in the distance, swelling like milk. All of a sudden they grew larger and turned black, a flash of lightning breaking out in their midst like a shooting star, followed by a low rumble of thunder. Over by their camp the weather was still nice and clear, flowers blooming everywhere, giving him a feeling of contentment much like the one he had had that morning.

"See—isn't it nice being on the high ground in the summer!" he announced to his wife with satisfaction. Looking around, he suddenly felt that some of their things hadn't been arranged quite right. Setting down his tea and getting to his feet, he switched around the satchel and the chest. Sadly, this arrangement seemed even less pleasing to the eye, so he picked the satchel back up, slid the chest back, placed the altar on top of the chest, and stashed the satchel down by its side. But this still didn't seem right at all, so he went back to pick up the satchel once again. The damn satchel, however, suddenly seemed so heavy that he couldn't pick it up, and he had to call his wife for help.

"*Ah tsi*, your temples are going gray!" His wife, completely taken aback, stared at him in amazement.

He raised his hand instinctively to feel his temples. "Your . . . your hair's . . . gone gray as well," he said. His wife too raised her hand instinctively to feel her hair, and let out a dejected sigh.

"The cows have all run off!" announced his son, as though he were issuing a command.

He raced after the cows as quickly as he could and finally managed to rein them all in. After taking a moment to catch his breath, he began herding the cows back. As he walked he mulled over the problem of finding a wife for his son, and before he knew it he'd arrived at the foot of the hill where their tent was pitched. The hill wasn't all that steep and it wasn't that far to the tent, but he felt exhausted, and on top of that he was getting battered by the autumn wind, dry grass whipping into his face. He simply had to sit down and rest for a while. When he did finally make it to the top of the hill, he felt a little better, but much to his surprise his wife and son had already pulled up the tent pegs and wound up the guide ropes, and were preparing to move camp.

"What are you doing?" he demanded, both disappointed and angry.

"Moving camp. If we don't move down to the valley for the winter this old tent'll get torn apart by the wind," said his son with a finality that brooked no discussion.

At that moment a scattered dusting of snowflakes began to fall from the freezing sky. His tattered jacket felt extremely light, and he couldn't help but shiver.

It was indeed warmer down in the valley, or at least the wind was less severe, and he felt a bit more at ease. But he really was unhappy with the placement of their possessions. Unfortunately, not only did he lack the strength to move them, he no longer had the authority to, so he had no choice but to put up with his discomfort. And so he chanted prayers to himself and continued to mull over the problem of finding a wife for his son.

In the glow cast by the flame of the stove, which gave them light and heat and cooked their food, he saw another fearful sight: his wife's face had become ridiculously small. Looking closer, he realized that she didn't have a tooth left in her mouth. Without thinking, he lifted his hand to feel his own face, and, sticking a finger into his mouth, he found nothing but a tongue. Feeling utterly dismal, he heaved a sigh.

In bed, he once again began to think about getting a wife for his son, but a sudden burst of joyous laughter cut off his train of thought. Pricking up his ears, he could make out one of the voices as his son's, and the voice of the other seemed to be that of a woman. The sound of the laughter woke up a child, who began to cry. The woman began to sing a lullaby: "Go to sleep, Mama's little darling, go to sleep and I'll get a horse for you, and we'll get a saddle for that horse, I'll pluck the stars from the sky for you, I'll pluck the flowers from the ground for you, go to sleep, Mama's little darling . . ."

Even he was lulled to sleep by the melody. He kept on rearranging the household possessions this way and that, but he could never get them the way he wanted. . . . His livestock ran off to someone else's land, and when he went to retrieve them he died by the blade of another's knife, and his son couldn't take revenge, couldn't even bring his body back. . . . All his hopes were entrusted to his grandson, whom he had taken on a pilgrimage to the Jowo in Lhasa. . . .

All night long, he was gripped by an endless stream of disjointed dreams.

9

THE HANDSOME MONK

ONE

Toward the end of the tenth month of the Tibetan calendar it snowed, making it feel even colder than the middle of winter. It got colder still at dusk, when thick black clouds gathered in the sky. Watching the sky over his home as he took a piss, Gendün Gyatso shivered involuntarily. He fastened his maroon-colored satin and lambskin jacket, thrust his hands inside the sleeves, and carried himself back to the camp with ponderous steps. A couple of seven-, maybe eight-year-old kids, each chewing on some roasted barley, ran over to greet him. "Akhu is here! I'll take your bag." Grabbing his yellow satchel, they wrestled and shoved their way inside.

With the exception of his sister-in-law, who was busy making *tsampa* by herself, there was no one at home. "Where's Mom gone?" asked Gendün Gyatso.

"She went to your sister's. She said she won't be back for a few days." His sister-in-law jumped up in a sudden fright. "Akhu, you look awful. Are you ill?"

When he heard these words, Gendün Gyatso's pounding heart settled somewhat. "No, no," he said. As he was about to sit, he heard from outside the simultaneous sounds of a neighing horse and the thud of a descending rider. "Dad's here!" cried the children in unison, wrestling and shoving their way out the door of the adobe house. His heart started pounding again.

"*Ah tsi*, you look terrible. Are you sick or something?" As soon as his brother, Gobha, saw him, he virtually yelled these words at Gendün Gyatso.

"No. I'm not . . . sick. I . . . you . . ."

"Me? I'm back from the front line to get provisions."

"Oh, the front . . . Was there an ambush?"

"Last night those bandits hit our second unit's camp again. By the grace of the Three Jewels, there were no casualties." Gobha moved to sit. "You really do look terrible. If you're not sick, then what's wrong?"

"There's . . . there's something I need to tell you . . ."

"Is that Gobha? Oh! And Akhu Gendün's here too!" An elderly neighbor entered Gobha's house, leaning on his walking stick. Both brothers rose.

"Please sit, Akhu Gendün, both of you please sit," urged the old man, himself taking a seat. From the way he tossed his walking stick to the floor with a clatter, you'd think he would never need it again. He seemed, however, to decide that this action was excessive, so he retrieved the stick and placed it in front of him. The walking stick made him seem very old, but he was in fact just over fifty, and his hair was still mostly black. Two years ago, during a pasture feud, he'd been shot in the calf, and because he couldn't get the wound treated right away, he'd been forced to rely on the walking stick ever since.

"Have the bandits hit again?"

"They hit our second unit's camp again last night. By the grace of the Three Jewels, there were no casualties. A cadre and a detachment of armed police are coming from the county today. Seems like the fighting will have to stop."

"Those bandits . . ." The old man impulsively pounded a fist onto his knee. A sharp pain shot up his leg, forcing an "Ow ow!" from his mouth. "Isn't there anything you can do to hit them back?" he asked, after a moment had passed.

"If they're not attacking, then that's a good thing. How can we attack them? We move about in the trenches all hunched over; if you peek your head over the top even a little bit, a thousand guns go off at once, like peas popping in a pan! You know all too well how good the bandits' weapons are." This last comment stirred in the old man feelings of terror, anguish, and hatred all at the same time. He bit his lip and fell silent. Gobha continued, "We're on the high ground, but apart from the slight advantage of terrain we've got nothing. Winter's coming, and the wind on the mountaintop is unbearable. Forget about fighting back—the men won't even be able to stand on their own two feet when that cold comes. We're in a real tight spot."

"Ah—it's not your fault. But those bandits have killed so many of our men. Even if we can't take revenge, we can't give them an inch of ground! If my leg wasn't like this, I'd throw these old bones into battle again! But without a penny, this is what happens . . ."

"How much are the yaks and sheep worth now?"

"Barely anything."

"*Eh*—well anyhow, if we don't sell some, we won't even be able to afford bullets."

"Oh, yeah—I've still got a few here. Take them. Kill a few of their men and horses. Even if you can't get revenge for your dad, you can put the fear into those bandits. I heard a Muslim came to Spearhead Gönpo's place selling guns and ammo for cheap. Where is Alak Drong now?" The old man suddenly turned to Gendün Gyatso. "It's your good karma that you monks don't have to lay eyes on the battlefield. It's no different from hell. If you hadn't taken your vows, you'd be out there now, feeling the terror and the pain—who knows, you might not even be alive. *Ah tsi*, our handsome monk is looking the worse for wear, is he unwell?"

Gendün Gyatso was a man with perfectly proportioned features. He had sleek black hair and a fair complexion. Just like in the Tibetan ode to Yangchen Lhamo, if you looked for a single fault on him, you'd simply be wasting your time. People called him "the handsome monk." His fellow monks had even said that, as he possessed the thirty-two auspicious marks and the eighty excellent signs of the Buddha, he must be the reincarnation of a great lama, and they entreated him to give them his blessing. These latter remarks might have been poking fun, but no one could deny the truth of the former. The women of Tsezhung joked about this topic in private: "If I could get Akhu Gendün to break his vows with me, spending the next life burning on the copper horse would be a small price to pay!" After everyone had had a good laugh, a penance would be added: "*Ah la*, only kidding, *om Vajrasattva*." When Gendün Gyatso was just six or seven years old, a lama visited his family. As soon as he saw Gendün Gyatso, he exclaimed in surprise. "*Ah tsi ah tsi*, what a remarkable boy! You must keep this child clean and healthy. . . . Mmm . . . it would be best if you have him enter the monkhood," he said, patting the boy's head. His father was overjoyed and before long sent him off to take his vows, but at no point had Gendün Gyatso displayed any remarkable characteristics. In any case, his handsome appearance and gentle character made up for the fact that he wasn't all that bright or hard-working, and he remained the object of people's desire and esteem.

Compared with those days, Gendün Gyatso really wasn't looking so good now. The most obvious change was in his face, which had completely lost its former luster. It had become ashen and gloomy, like that of a man in very poor health. And the conversation his brother had had with that damn neighbor had heaped fresh suffering on his suffering, and fresh terror on his terror. He tried to get his emotions under control and calm himself down, but as soon as he stopped concentrating on it he began hyperventilating. That night he couldn't get to sleep at all, and the next day he looked even worse. "You really do look terrible," his brother said. "Go and see Alak Drong, or a doctor. There's definitely something wrong." He stuffed some money into his hand and left.

Gendün Gyatso put a hand to his face, then set out after his brother, who was already astride his horse.

"Oh, right," said his brother, suddenly reining in his mount. "Wasn't there something you wanted to tell me?"

Gendün Gyatso's heart almost leaped into his throat, and he felt like he could barely breathe. "I . . . I mean . . . you . . . you should . . . be careful, be on your guard," he said, swallowing repeatedly.

"That's it?"

"No, I mean, yes, ah . . . that's it."

"Don't worry yourself."

As he watched his brother ride away, Gendün Gyatso thought, *It's best to just get it over with, like pulling a tooth—do it in one go. Worse comes to worst, I'd get a crack of his whip. And maybe I'd be feeling a bit better right now if I'd done it.* He sighed, regretting that he hadn't dared tell his brother what was really on his mind.

TWO

At dusk, Gendün Gyatso returned to the county seat. Wrapping his robe around his head, he wandered the streets aimlessly. That morning he'd eaten a simple breakfast, and though he hadn't had a bite to eat for lunch or dinner, he didn't feel hungry at all. When darkness fell, he found himself wandering unconsciously back into the Red Lantern Bar. Alcohol can relieve your troubles, they say, so maybe a drink would help.

A young woman came over and sat beside him. "You're still wearing your monk's robes," she whispered.

"Go away. Bring me a beer."

The woman stood up, shocked. A moment later she sat again. "If you want to drink, you can come to my place."

Gendün Gyatso had no desire whatsoever to return to the woman's place, so he rose and walked out the door. When he came back to the bar some two or three hours later, he was more or less drunk. Not only had the alcohol failed to ease his pain, it had aroused in him a strong desire to be with the woman again. In fact, even in the midst of the intense anguish and fear of the last few days, he hadn't been able to put her out of his mind. Sometimes he hated the woman, sometimes he loved her. In the end, he himself couldn't say for sure; all he knew was that he had an irrepressible desire to be with her. The woman really seemed to like him too. At the start she'd told him, quite candidly, "As a woman doing a job like this, I go with whoever pays me, but I've never met a man as handsome as you before. To tell you the truth, I really like you. But I've never made a monk break his vows, and there's no way I'm starting now. It looks to me like you're no ordinary monk. I think it'd be best if you just forgot all about this kind of thing."

At that moment Gendün Gyatso had been overcome by a wave of desire, his sole wish being to bed the woman on the spot. Even if he'd had to die and go to hell as soon as he'd had her, it would have been worth it. "I already gave up my vows," he'd lied.

"Then what are you doing still wearing monk's robes?"

"I only gave them up yesterday. I don't have any other clothes right now. I'm planning to go home and get my lay clothes tomorrow."

"Why don't you get some Chinese clothes? Aren't a lot of former monks wearing Chinese clothes these days?"

"I've never worn Chinese clothes in my life, and I don't intend to wear them now. Stop delaying."

The woman had point-blank refused the money he'd offered, and Gendün Gyatso had felt moved. "A pretty, nice girl like you shouldn't be working in a place like this. I hope you find yourself a husband and get on the right track," he'd said then, and meant it.

"A girl who's done this job can never find a husband, especially a good one," she'd said with a sigh.

"A monk and a prostitute. Aren't we the perfect match?" He'd then told her a true story about a monk from his monastery who went back to lay life. After giving up his vows, he married a prostitute, and they even had children.

"You're making fun of me."

Even he hadn't known if he was kidding or being serious. Either way, he would have to return home the next day and get back into his fur jacket—there was no avoiding that. But he had gradually begun to feel a profound sense of regret, mostly because he hadn't considered that shedding his monk's robes meant he would have to go to the front line, where the most he had to look forward to was seeking revenge for his father. Ever since he was a child he'd been used to the warmth of the monks' quarters. Even when he returned to the family tent he lay in bed miserably, unable to stand the cold. If there was one thing more unbearable to him than fighting, it was sitting on a mountaintop thirteen thousand feet above sea level, getting blasted by freezing winds. What's more, even when the fighting was over, he'd still have to be out in the wind and the rain tending the cattle. He'd have to stalk about like a wolf just for the sake of keeping his belly full—this, like the breaking of his vows, was already a fact. When you think of it like that, how you can say all those clever people who leave their homes and renounce worldly affairs to pursue a life of solitude are doing it just for the welfare of sentient beings? And those soldiers who flee the battlefield and face disdain and ridicule, and then the next damn life . . .

"*Ah kha*, what an idiot I am!" Gendün Gyatso had been tormented with regret. "Demon, you wicked demon, look what you've done to me . . ." He'd wept bitterly, striking himself in the chest over and over.

"Didn't you say you already gave up your vows?"

"I was lying to you. I was lying to myself."

"*Ah ho*, you've ruined me! What will I do in the next life!?"

"Prostitutes don't have anything to look forward to in the next life anyway. You'll be spending the next life knee-deep in shit, piss, pus, and blood."

The woman didn't get mad, she'd simply cried and leaned her head against Gendün Gyatso. "I have no regrets. I have no regrets."

"Me neither." Gendün Gyatso had put his arm around her neck. These weren't just words, either. It was too late now anyway, he'd thought, there was no use in having regrets. He was by no means the only one to forsake his vows, and what's more, this woman was a real beauty—the most beautiful thing in the world is a woman, after all. Haven't plenty of people given up their lives for the sake of a woman? Despite this, it wasn't long before he felt regret again, and it came most notably whenever he sobered up— *What have I done?* he would chastise himself. Soon after that, the unstoppable regret and fear came back, so he kept drinking, trying his best to forget it all.

THREE

There's a new saying: "Most men are called Tashi, and most Tashis are businessmen; most women are called Lhamo, and most Lhamos are prostitutes." But the name of the woman Gendün Gyatso was in love with wasn't Lhamo, it was Lhatso. Lhatso rented a small room behind the Red Lantern Bar. Half of the room was taken up by a large bed, at the head of which was a cupboard. In addition to some makeup, the cupboard contained a yellow book called *The Lineage of Nyizer Monastery*. The book was distinctly out of place in that room, and it piqued Gendün Gyatso's curiosity. He asked Lhatso where it came from.

"A client left it here by accident a few days ago. Said he was a tourist. I was going to throw it out, but it's full of pictures of lamas and the monastery, so I kept it."

Though the room looked very clean, it had a foul odor. Gendün Gyatso suspected that it might be the smell of semen. He lit incense again and again, but the smell proved hard to get rid of. For that reason, he spent less and less time in the little room and began to roam between other bars, clubs, and especially video stores. Though those places too had their share of pretty "Lhamos," in his eyes none of them was as pretty or as kindhearted as Lhatso. Every evening, when he finished his drifting, he ended up back at Lhatso's, and he was usually drunk. At first he cursed her, calling her a "black-hearted woman" and an "evil woman," then he cried and struck himself in the chest with his fist. *I can't go on like this . . . what's the point of living . . .* he thought sometimes, and even considered suicide.

"If you want to die, do it somewhere else," said Lhatso, at the end of her tether. Then she held him. "Please, don't torture yourself like this. You're not the only one to break his vows. Even lamas break their vows, never mind ordinary monks. They don't have any regrets, so why should you? Get rid of your robes and give up the drink. We can open up a little store or a guesthouse together." She tried to console him with these and other heartfelt words.

"No, no, you know nothing! If I give up my robes I'll be forced to get a gun and go to the front line, and the man who killed my father is there, so I'll have to be out in front, and those bandits have the better weapons . . . oh—you know nothing . . ."

"So . . . it's like that."

"It's like that. I'm not just a fallen monk, I'm a coward too. Now you know."

"Then . . . why don't we go to my hometown?"

"Didn't you say you're from Chukar County?"

"Yes."

"Haha—that's exactly where the man who killed my father is. They're still fighting with our camp now."

"Oh . . . I see. Then why don't we go somewhere else?"

Gendün Gyatso shook his head, not wanting to talk anymore, and went to sleep.

Every morning, Gendün Gyatso read *The Lineage of Nyizer Monastery* in bed, both to forget his troubles and to pass the day. The book documented a lineage of abbots from a Nyingma monastery in Kham. The photos of Nyizer Tsang, the great lama in charge of the monastery, looked just like him. Nyizer Tsang had died at the age of twenty-five, which, counting back from now, was twenty-five years ago—the year before Gendün Gyatso was born. The book said that the huge boulder into which he drove a ritual dagger was now the monastery's most precious religious artifact.

Though the features of the handsome monk Gendün Gyatso had lost their former luster, his sleek, black hair had grown long, and anyone who saw him still felt that he was something special. When he was playing pool or watching a dirty movie at the video place, or whenever he was drunk, he always attracted a lot of attention. For that reason he didn't want to go out anymore, and he kept swearing to himself that he wouldn't. Nevertheless, spending day and night in Lhatso's tiny, semen-stinking room was, to him, no different from being in prison. "They say samsara is the prison of demons—how true," he finally said to himself, and walked out the door. First he went to a pool courtyard—one of his old haunts from before he broke his vows. Hardly anyone in the little county seat was a match for him now, so he didn't even have to waste any money. He didn't give his opponent the slightest chance, and his mood lifted with the ringing clack of each potted ball. But soon a crowd of people gathered around him, staring in wonder. Feeling deeply uncomfortable, he quit his game, and wrapping his robe up over his head left the courtyard. When he was drunk, however, he was never so cautious. He staggered about like the flame of a butter lamp in the wind, sometimes treading on his trailing robe and sending himself head over heels, after which he lay there, crawling about and rambling incomprehensibly. Sometimes he stuffed his fingers into his mouth, trying to make himself throw up. If not that, he moaned pitifully, or just lay flat on his back and passed out. If people gathered around to stare at him, he rolled about on the ground, shouting, "What are you looking at? We're all people! Am I the only monk who drinks? Am I the only monk who's broken his vows? Ya, *hic* . . . Alak Drong smokes, and drinks, and he's got a wife, and a kid, *hic* . . . and he's still wearing the crown of the five Buddhas, and giving empowerments and transmissions and instructions! Ah, *hic* . . . you want to see a show, go see that! Ah . . . go on, go!" With that he flailed his arms, shooing them off.

"What a disgrace, what a fraud!" "Outrageous, absolutely outrageous," "I swear on the *Kangyur*, if he wasn't wearing monk's robes, I'd sort him out"—the crowd cursed him with indignant oaths.

Luckily, Lhatso came running over at just that moment. She heaved Gendün Gyatso into her rented motor trike, got him home, and laid him on the bed. Not only did she clean the vomit off his clothes, she shook the dirt out of them too. His ice-cold heart was thawed by the warm tenderness of a woman, and he burst into tears. "Let's get married, we have to get married!" he blurted out.

Lhatso was used to hearing such things. "Go to sleep. We'll talk about marriage when you sober up," she said.

In the morning, when Gendün Gyatso had sobered up, the foul odor of semen again drifted into his nostrils, and all talk of marriage was dropped. Feeling ashamed of his embarrassing behavior the night before, he leafed through the pages of *The Lineage of*

Nyizer Monastery. He more or less knew the slim volume by heart now and had no desire to read it in detail. He breathed a long sigh and finally got out of bed.

FOUR

The weather grew colder by the day, and now it was freezing even at noon. Sometimes a wind blew in from who knows where and tossed the white plastic trash discarded on the streets to and fro.

A young nomad who was revving the engine of his motorbike and charging aimlessly up and down the street suddenly collided with a pig, sending the bike skidding off a good ten paces. The rider, after flying five or six paces into the air, landed on the back of another pig that at that moment just happened to emerge from underneath the toilets. Happily, the man was unhurt and the bike undamaged, but the young man now smelled as unbearably awful as the pig he'd just hit. The onlookers, covering their noses with their hands, backed off as they burst into laughter.

Gendün Gyatso too chuckled to himself as he watched this spectacle. That was the first time he'd broken into a smile since forsaking his vows. Unfortunately, it only lasted for a moment, as a group of young monks—their robes wrapped over their heads, revealing only their eyes—was scrutinizing him suspiciously.

Since it was the cold season and the weather was so bad, Gendün Gyatso decided not to go to the pool courtyard and went straight into a bar instead. The monks who were tailing him didn't come into the bar but went to a restaurant across the road, where they looked in his direction through the window.

When Gendün Gyatso staggered out the door it was almost five in the morning. There was a fierce wind blowing and hardly anyone was around. The monks who had been watching him wrapped their robes over their heads, exited the restaurant, and blocked his path. "Akhu, your robe has fallen on the floor," said one of the monks as he picked up a corner of the robe and wrapped it over Gendün Gyatso's head, covering his face.

The bewildered Gendün Gyatso wanted to remove the robe from his eyes, but someone had his hands in a tight grip and he was unable to move. He hadn't a clue what was going on, and before he had the chance to react he was being dragged in an unknown direction. He shouted and screamed, but his voice was so inaudible in the harsh wind that he could barely hear it himself. He struggled as hard as he could, but the men holding him from either side were as firm as mountains, and he wasn't able to move them an inch.

The night before he had had a dream. Several monks took him by force to a large assembly hall, or maybe the residence of Alak Drong. They savagely stripped off his clothes, leaving him naked. Using a wooden spoon, Alak Drong inspected his genitals at great length, and finally, letting out a laugh, proclaimed, "He hasn't broken his vows!"

The monks released him at once, and with exceptional reverence, begged his pardon as they re-dressed him.

He was overcome with joy and was so moved that he wept. Realizing that he really hadn't broken his vows, he became even more overjoyed. But he didn't want to leave Lhatso, so he hugged her tightly. This had woken her up, and she'd shouted in order to wake him. He'd been feverish and dripping with sweat, and had once more fallen into the abyss of suffering.

He'd been having so many dreams like this lately. Was this a dream too? Or had the Lord of Death's messengers already brought him to the next life? *No, no,* he thought once more, *even if I can't see it, I'm still in the human world, for sure. Maybe someone's playing a joke on me?* At that moment they stopped, and someone said to him, "Hey—people break their vows, but who keeps on wearing monk's robes after they do? Why are you still dressed like a monk?"

The wind must have calmed down all of a sudden, as he could hear everything distinctly.

A man whose voice sounded just like that of a woman seized him by the scruff of the neck. "What is the meaning of defiling the robes of the Buddhist order like this? Have you got some kind of problem with Buddhist robes?"

Gendün Gyatso, now even more convinced that this was neither a dream nor the afterlife, wanted to say something, but his assailant now grabbed him by the throat. "You bastard, badmouthing Alak Drong! Let's see you get out of this!" With that the man punched him in the face. White, red, and yellow filled his vision all at once, and he tasted blood in his mouth.

"You still dare to slander Alak Drong now, huh?" said someone else as he punched him fiercely in the solar plexus. His whole body turned to jelly and he collapsed helplessly on the ground, feeling like his guts had been shredded.

"Take this, you fraud!" With a crack, a hard object connected with the back of Gendün Gyatso's head, and he passed out.

Although it was completely dark by the time Gendün Gyatso regained consciousness, he could tell by the faint moonlight that he was in a narrow alleyway. He felt cold, his head ached, he was thirsty, and his mouth tasted of blood. After a moment, he touched his hand to his head, and it came back covered in something wet and sticky—blood, of course—and he panicked. Mustering all his strength, he tried to get up, but his head felt even heavier than his body. In the end, his limbs unable to support him, he slumped back on the ground. He touched his hand to his head again. Blood was still trickling down the back of his neck from a wound the size of two fingers put together, causing him even greater alarm.

Going to the front line can't be any worse than this. I ought to just get rid of these robes now, thought Gendün Gyatso as he pressed his forehead to the ground and lay there moaning in pain. Hearing the sound of footsteps, he raised his head slightly with the aid of his hands. As the footsteps approached the beam of a flashlight fell on him, and a man cried out, "*Ah tsi!* Someone's collapsed here!"

"*Ah tsi ah tsi*, it's a monk!" yelled the voice of a woman.

Gendün Gyatso told them that he'd been robbed and asked them to call a motor trike for him. Not only did they call one, they wanted to accompany him to the hospital as well, but he declined.

After they set off, Gendün Gyatso said to the trike driver, "Take me to the Red Lantern Bar."

"What? That's no place for a monk. I think you should go to the hospital."

"Just do what I said."

FIVE

Gendün Gyatso put on the Chinese clothes that Lhatso had bought for him and combed his hair, and he looked just as handsome as when he was a monk. But the pain in his head refused to go away, and sometimes he felt so dizzy he almost collapsed. Lhatso, helping to support him, took him to the hospital.

When they got to the hospital yard there were a lot more people than usual. Some were crying, some were standing in a daze, and some were pursuing the doctors who were rushing back and forth. Gendün Gyatso paid no attention to these people. Keeping his head lowered like a thief, he crept into the outpatient department. There were people lying left and right on the floor of the corridor, moaning horribly. An old man had been shot in the right side of his chest, and as he breathed red bubbles were sucked in and blown out of the hole. Near him was a man of about twenty with a wound bursting out of his left shoulder, like a blooming flower. The frozen hell where human beings split open like lotuses must be precisely like this, Gendün Gyatso thought. "Blessed Three Jewels," he murmured. This was the first prayer he had uttered since breaking his vows. A man with a belt bound around his head shivered fearfully and took a few gulps of air, as though he'd suddenly plunged into a freezing pool of water in the middle of winter, then fell still. The man who'd been holding his head in his lap shook him, calling out, "Sangbha, Sangbha," then, raising his voice, began to shout, "Doctor! *Ah ho!* Doctor! Where's the doctor? Doc—tor—," but no one answered him. He leaned the man—or rather, corpse—against a wall, and after rushing from room to room finally managed to track down a doctor, whom he dragged over forcibly. The doctor, without removing his left hand from the pocket of his lab coat, used the thumb and index finger of his right hand to open the eyes of the man—whose head had by now slumped onto his shoulder—and gave him a quick glance. He put his fingers briefly to the man's neck and said, "He's gone."

The man seized the doctor. "What do you mean?" he cried, wide-eyed.

"He's gone. Stopped breathing."

The man slowly released the doctor and, as though he had suddenly thought of something, began to shout, "Friends! Friends! Where is Alak Drong? Where is Alak Drong?," but no one answered him. Then a man whose voice sounded just like that of a woman ran over, crying, "Doctor! Doctor! Come quick!" as he pulled and tugged at the doctor's sleeve. The man's unusual voice stirred something in Gendün Gyatso's memory. When he looked closely he discovered, as if awaking from a dream, that those people were in fact all from his camp. The man who had just died with his head slumped on his shoulder was Sanggyé Kyab, the boy who used to tend cattle with him when they were children.

Gendün Gyatso suddenly remembered his brother and began rushing madly about. The doctor from before was now in the middle of giving oxygen to a wounded man. The man was lying face up on a stretcher. As he was covered by a woolen coat, his wound couldn't be seen, but the whites of his rolled-back eyeballs were visible, and a coarse, drawn-out grunt was coming from his throat, just like that made by a cow when a Muslim butcher slits its throat.

Gendün Gyatso said another prayer, then continued to search each and every corridor and room. Much to his relief, not only was there no sign of his brother Gobha, he didn't find any of his other relatives either. He thought about checking whether anyone else had been wounded, but recalling his own circumstances, he decided this wasn't a place he should linger in and beat a hasty exit through the hospital doors. Outside, he let out a deep breath and finally slowed his pace.

"What's going on?" demanded a terrified Lhatso, planting herself in front of Gendün Gyatso.

"This is the work of your Chukar County."

"Blessed Jetsün Drölma!"

"If they find out you're from Chukar County, they'll skin you alive."

"And who could blame them? I'm scared."

"I'm scared too. Really scared."

"These pasture feuds are so horrible."

"I guess this is what they call the cycle of samsara."

After he'd received that beating, Gendün Gyatso had vowed that he would shed his monk's robes and give up the drink. *I may have broken my vows*, he'd thought, *but it's not right to defile the Buddhist garments, and I'd have fewer regrets going to the front line than living like this—neither monk nor layman, neither man nor demon.* So he'd removed his robes. But after he witnessed the terrifying scenes at the hospital, his courage again vanished. As soon as he got to Lhatso's place, he put his robes back on. Anxious about his brother and his family and disgusted by his own behavior, his mind was beset as though by a storm and he couldn't calm down. Eventually, he called to Lhatso and asked her to go get him some beer.

"Shouldn't you not be drinking? And we don't have much money left, either."

Gendün Gyatso knew that since Lhatso had met him she had of her own accord cut off all contact with other men, and she paid for the rent, the food, and moreover his booze and his clothes. With this in mind, he heaved a sigh. "You're right. That damn money . . ."

Lhatso seemingly wanted to give him some comfort. "Oh, well, there's still enough to buy a bit of beer. I'll go get some," she said, rising to leave.

"No, no, I don't want any now. And I won't drink in the future either. Promise."

SIX

Without his realizing it, the smell of semen completely disappeared, and he developed a sense of familiarity with and attachment to the room as if it were his own home.

As it happened, the cadre with a face whiter than paper, who came almost every week to the Red Lantern Bar and stayed there for free, was a policeman. At midday he came to the Red Lantern Bar in full policeman's uniform and whispered a few words into the ear of the woman who owned the place. After he left, the owner gathered all of the "Lhamos" and announced, "The police are going to raid us tonight. Be careful, and only standard services—no entertaining clients." This forced Gendün Gyatso to go spend the night in a hotel.

When we Tibetans go to the city, the hotels put us all in the same room, and in the same way, the hotels in this county seat put monks in the same room. The room that Gendün Gyatso was put into contained two old monks. They said they were from Kham.

"Have you ever been to Nyizer Monastery?" asked Gendün Gyatso idly.

"We are *from* Nyizer Monastery, as it happens."

Gendün Gyatso became immediately enthused. "Oh! Tell me, is the boulder that Nyizer Tsang drove a ritual dagger into still there?"

One of the old monks leaped up all of a sudden, and whispered to his colleague, "Hey, look closely. He . . ." Turning back to Gendün Gyatso, he asked, "Have you ever been to Nyizer Monastery, sir?"

"No."

"May we inquire as to your age, sir?"

"I'm twenty-five."

The two old monks sat there agape, now glancing at each other, now staring at Gendün Gyatso. "You . . ." said Gendün Gyatso, feeling somewhat uncomfortable. The two monks returned to their senses. One of them began to frantically search through his backpack, and after some time retrieved a photograph. He brought it over to Gendün Gyatso with extreme care.

Gendün Gyatso took a look at the photo and said, "Yes, that's Nyizer Tsang."

The two old monks gawked at each other and fell completely silent. After a moment the elder of the two began to babble incoherently, and upon failing to express anything resembling a point, awkwardly wiped the sweat dripping down his brow and the tip of his nose, after which he continued to babble even more incoherently than before. The other, slightly younger monk cut him off and got straight to the point. "Would it be acceptable if we looked at the back of your head, sir?" he asked.

Gendün Gyatso wondered if he had fallen into one of those unpleasant illusions or dreams again. He unconsciously felt the scar on the back of his head and stared in amazement at the two monks sitting before him, one after the other.

"Um . . . speaking plainly, the Nyizer incarnations all have a dragon pattern on the back of their heads."

Gendün Gyatso felt the back of his head again, understanding everything clearly now. But strangely, he suddenly became even more flustered than the two old monks. "No, no, it's not a dragon pattern!" he cried, jumping to his feet.

The two old monks nodded to each other and pounced on Gendün Gyatso like madmen. He wailed in anguish and struggled as hard as he could, but he fell into their grasp as if bound by the noose of the Dharma protectors. After they had taken a look at the back of his head, they suddenly let him go. "Well, there's no doubt now," said one to the other.

"Lamas, *yidams, dakinis*, and Dharma protectors! Our task is finally complete." The slightly younger of the two monks prostrated to Gendün Gyatso three times, and as his head touched Gendün Gyatso's feet, he wept tears of joy.

The elder monk too prostrated three times, then placed a stack of money on top of a *khata* and brought it before Gendün Gyatso, who became even more flustered and terrified. "No, no, you've made a mistake! I'm not a *trülku*, it's not possible!" he yelped. He went so far as to tell them, quite plainly, that he wasn't even a genuine monk. The two old monks didn't hear a word he said; instead they began to tell him about how before his death the previous Nyizer incarnation had composed a final testament, which clearly stated that there was no need to look for his reincarnation for twenty-five years, that his reincarnation would then be twenty-five years old, where they should search, and so on. "Please, don't talk like that anymore," they said. "Please come back to your monastery at once."

Gendün Gyatso had no idea how to explain the situation to them, and it looked like the two monks were so insistent that they wouldn't give him the chance to do so anyway. "Why don't you get up? We'll talk about this later," he said with resignation, making them sit back on the bed. "I've got a wife," he added with a sigh.

The two monks took one look at each other and, almost in unison, replied, "The Nyizer incarnations have always had consorts."

"But my wife is a . . . and I'm a drunk too."

"The Nyizer incarnations have always partaken of the elixirs."

Gendün Gyatso's mind was in turmoil. *What's going on?* he thought. *Is this all just a coincidence?* All of a sudden he thought of Lhatso and felt an irrepressible urge to see her. Hitching up his cassock, he bolted out the door and tore off. The two old monks went after him like cops chasing a criminal.

A crowd had gathered at the doorway of the Red Lantern Bar. Two policemen roughly shoved Lhatso into their car, then sped off to the piercing blare of the siren.

Gendün Gyatso stared after the police car, stupefied.

That day was the coldest of the year in the county seat. On the mountain peaks thirteen thousand feet above sea level, it was probably even colder.

10

REVENGE

Since the stern, swarthy face of our clan leader was never graced by even the hint of a smile, he gave people the impression of being very fearsome. But in reality he was a man who only ever thought of the well-being of his people, so he was respected by all.

When that swarthy face came in through the door of our home, Mother and I leaped up in a flash to offer him the seat of honor, but without saying a word he motioned for me to come outside. Like a servant, I bowed my head and followed him. When we had gotten far enough away that Mother couldn't hear us, the clan leader turned suddenly and said, "Boy, your father's killer is in my house at this very moment."

My heart began to pound intensely, and I had to keep swallowing my saliva.

"But the man is my friend. I trust that you won't cause any problems." As soon as the words were out of his mouth, he took off without giving me the chance to respond.

I had heard that my father's killer was the leader of the clan from across the river. He was brave and brutal. He had killed many people, but not once had he paid the price for it. My father had relied on stealing to make his living; apart from the meager renown that came with being called a brave lad, he didn't have a thing to his name. In the winter that I turned nine, Father crossed the frozen river to go steal from the clan on the other side. Unfortunately, he fell into their hands, and after subjecting him to unimaginable torments, the clan leader himself killed my father and threw his body onto the river ice. Since my family was so poor back then, people felt bad that such a terrible thing had befallen us and everyone consoled and helped us as much as they could, especially our clan leader. He went across the river again and again to seek compensation and did his very best to look after my mother and me. But by the time I was fifteen or sixteen, we still hadn't received any compensation, let alone taken revenge for my father's murder, and as a result I became a target for mockery and abuse. More and more people began to openly insult me. "The father was a meat-eating vulture, but the son's a shit-eating crow," they said. It got to the point that I couldn't hold my head up among the young men of the clan.

Ah! Were the Dharma protectors looking out for me today, bringing the lamb to the mouth of the wolf's den? Or was it to be the day that I followed in my father's footsteps? Either way, if I didn't grasp an opportunity like this with both hands, I'd have no right to call myself my father's son, and I'd be even more frozen out of the community.

"The look on your face! What did the clan leader say to you?" As soon as I came back inside my mother seized my hand with an anxious expression.

"Nothing. It's nothing. He just asked me to help him with something," I said, picking up the worn-out knife from where it hung on the side of the tent. Removing it from its sheath, I began to sharpen it vigorously on the grindstone. Mother became even more agitated, praying desperately to the goddess Tara while beseeching me, almost in tears. "There's definitely something going on. If you won't tell me what it is, I'll go ask the clan leader myself!"

It looked like I couldn't keep it a secret anymore. I stopped sharpening the knife and told her the truth. Much to my surprise, Mother calmed down. "Oh, there really is such a thing as karma! Your dear old father used to say that you've got to be brave when that crucial moment arrives, and you've got to be even more quick-witted. Remember that well. That's all I have to say." She then began to chant the "Ode to Tara" as though nothing were the matter.

I sharpened the old knife until it was like a razor, then stashed it in my sleeve. With all my might I tried to suppress my madly pounding heartbeat, and adopting a calm and collected air, I entered the home of the clan leader. The first thing that appeared before me was a woman making *tsampa*. The white *tsampa* flour was piled up almost three inches high all around the blue mill-stone. Sitting carefree atop the stove was a powerful-looking man whose braid, face, neck . . . well, in short, whose whole body radiated a glossy sheen as though he'd been sprinkled all over with oil. This was surely the man who had killed my father.

May the deities and the Dharma protectors come to my aid tonight! With this prayer in my mind, I rushed forward and plunged the knife as hard as I could into the right side of the man's chest. Without pulling out the blade I drove it further in, and from his insides I could hear the cracking sound of either flesh, muscle, or bone splitting apart. As the man's eyeballs bulged, he gradually fell back onto the floor. Then, withdrawing the knife and grasping the handle with both hands, I continued to stab him indiscriminately. Blood spurted from each of the wounds like a fountain and covered my entire face in a shower of droplets, turning it warm.

At that moment I heard a piercing cry. Turning around, I saw the woman who had been making *tsampa* scurrying out of the door on all fours.

I continued to stab the knife into his body—or corpse—over and over, just like I used to aimlessly stick my spade into a pile of fresh dung when I was a child. Eventually I no longer had the energy to pull the knife out and was panting so hard I could barely breathe. A searing pain raged in my head, and I felt nauseated. The earth was shaking and the sky was spinning, and I had no choice but to stop. *It turns out killing someone is more painful than being killed,* I thought.

Leaning my weight on the handle of the knife, I breathed heavily. When I looked at the man—the corpse—before me, all I could see in his wide-open eyes was glistening white, not a hint of black at all.

His sleek, oily braid, his face, his neck—his whole body was now completely covered in blood. Now that I thought about it, the first time I stabbed him I must have hit his heart or severed an artery, since the whole time he hadn't even reached for the knife hanging at his waist, let alone unsheathed it.

As I wiped the blood from my eyes and staggered out the door, I caught a blurry glimpse of the killer's blood seeping into the white *tsampa* by the millstone, turning it red and causing it to drip down the side. Just then the clan leader returned home. His swarthy face surveyed the entire room before he calmly proceeded over to the body, where he briefly checked the killer's pulse like a doctor examining a patient. "How could someone who killed one of my people ever be my friend?" he said as he closed the man's eyelids.

This was nine years after my father's murder, in the winter of the year I turned eighteen. The clan leader had some men come to take the killer's body and throw it on the frozen river. I felt like a man who'd just been released from prison.

Ever since then, I've had the respect of everyone in the clan, so much so that when important clan business is being discussed I always get called to the meetings. The sad thing is that my thoughts have begun to weigh heavily on my mind, to the point that I can hardly get a good night's sleep. From what I've heard, my father's killer had a nine-year-old son. Now I am his father's killer. I should get married as soon as possible, so that when I die by his knife, I'll have someone to take revenge for me.

11

NOSE RINGS

ONE

"Touch your head and feel nothing but hair; touch your feet and feel nothing but nails." Once again, this saying aptly described the situation Dukkar Tsering found himself in: he didn't have a thing to his name. He was staggering back home from the county seat as though weighed down by a thousand-pound burden. And in fact, the tens of thousands of yuan he'd borrowed from the bank wasn't just a thousand-pound burden to a poor nomad family like his, it was something that was of no benefit to him personally and did nothing to appease his creditors, either. Thinking of all this now, the young man who'd just turned thirty, his limbs all muscle, felt tears of remorse welling unstoppably at the corners of his eyes.

The tips of all sorts of plants were escaping from their prisons of ice and poking up through the soil, birds of all kinds were soaring in the sky singing their melodious tunes, and the air was pervaded by the earthy fragrance of soil. The glory of spring had arrived in the world of man. From some unknown source there came the love song of a young woman:

From the flocks that side of the Machu
I hear the cuckoo's beautiful song,
and my heart is so happy.
From the tents this side of the Machu
I hear my sweetheart's beautiful voice,
and my heart is so happy.

None of this, however, had any effect on Dukkar Tsering, who continued to press arduously onward, step after heavy step. All he could see was the symbols on mahjong tiles, and all he could hear was the clacking sound of the tiles being shuffled. What a horrible, despicable feeling! He bit his lip, tears once more welling at the corners of his eyes. His vision now blurred, he came to a halt and sat down on the ground.

I'm not a man. I can't go home now. How can I show my face to my family . . . ah ho . . . *what have I done . . .* Dukkar Tsering beat his chest as he admonished himself. He felt a sudden craving for a cigarette and stuck his hand in his pocket, but he couldn't even find a match, let alone a cigarette. Feeling even lower now, he hung his head and said to himself, *Tens of thousands of yuan, gone again just like that? Impossible. I'm not a man, I'm a dog. Worse than a dog.*

"Ah, kind sirs, I have asked you to come here today because my good-for-nothing bum of a son has been gambling again, and he's lost tens of thousands. We're all out of grain, and my daughter-in-law took the two kids and left. So . . . so I ask you all to please take pity on us—again." Dukkar Tsering's father opened the meeting with these preliminary remarks, although, bluntly put, they would be more accurately described as begging.

"But this time Dukkar Tsering needs to swear in front of all of us that he won't gamble again. 'A man won't swallow his oath, and a dog won't swallow metal.'"

"That's right. It wasn't just once or twice. If he keeps gambling like this he won't just ruin your family, he'll ruin our whole camp. He has to swear in front of all of us, right here and now, that he won't gamble anymore. If he does that, then we'll do whatever we can to help him again."

"That's right, that's right . . ." The other members of the community voiced their complete agreement with the opinions of the two speakers.

Dukkar Tsering, who had been hanging his head since the start of the meeting, was left with no choice. "If I gamble again, then I'm not a man, I'm a dog," he vowed, feebly.

The community persuaded Dukkar Tsering's wife to come back home and bailed him out with donations: some gave a yak, some gave a *dri*, some gave a ram, and some gave a ewe. In the morning he herded them to the county seat, where he sold them for over thirty thousand yuan.

His original plan was to go straight to the bank and pay down at least half his debt, then go to the market and buy some grain, which he would transport back home with a rented tractor. Yet, as soon as the money was in his hands, he was pulled by a strange and irresistible force that wouldn't allow him to go to the bank or to the grain market, a force that pulled him—without even giving him the chance to remember the business about the "man" and the "dog"—straight to a club run by a local police chief, where signs in Tibetan and Chinese on all four walls read "Gambling Prohibited."

TWO

At dusk, a man riding a black horse caught up to Dukkar Tsering. It was Orgyen, an old man from their camp. Orgyen was over sixty years old, thin and dark skinned, and he wore a ragged fur-lined coat. He wasn't a man anyone wanted to pay much attention to. "Is that Dukbhé? You look terrible. Have you been gambling again?"

This was the last thing Dukkar Tsering wanted to hear at that moment, and it made him feel both nervous and irritated. "No," he snapped, offering the old man no other greeting. His attitude, however, already provided clear proof that Dukkar Tsering not only had been gambling but also had lost. Orgyen launched into an interminable lecture about the fate of opium smokers and gambling addicts in both the old and new societies, about how Dukkar Tsering used to be such a good boy and used to be so considerate to others before he fell under the spell of gambling, but now people wouldn't class him in the rank of dogs, let alone the ranks of men, and so on and on.

Dukkar Tsering grew even more irritated. He halted, at the end of his tether now, and as he blankly looked Orgyen up and down he noticed the edges of a few bread cakes sticking out of the man's pocket. His face turned pale and his body trembled. He realized that he hadn't had a thing to eat since yesterday morning and was struck by a sudden and intense pang of hunger. Worse than that, he remembered how before he left for the county seat yesterday his eighty-year-old grandma had extracted a five-yuan note from beneath layers and layers of packaging, placed it in his hands, and instructed him to bring back a few bread cakes. When his older sister, who'd married into another community, had heard that he'd fallen into debt again, she'd come to help out, bearing some butter and cheese and leading two yaks. She had wailed bitterly the whole time, pleading repeatedly with him not to gamble anymore, and just before she left, she'd given that five-yuan note to his grandma.

Ah ho, what am I going to give to Grandma now? I'm not a man, I'm a dog. Worse than a dog . . .

Old man Orgyen was still advising and admonishing, but not a word of it was registering with Dukkar Tsering, whose eyes were still fixed like arrows on the bread cakes in Orgyen's pocket. He thought, *All I'd have to do is stick out my hand, pull the old man off the horse, press him to the ground, and wring his neck, just like that, and in the time it takes to drink a cup of tea those bread cakes would be mine! And if I were lucky he might have a good bit of money on him too. Yes, on the surface all he's got is that ragged old fur coat, but don't these types always skimp on their food and save on their drink, then end up hoarding loads of cash? Plus it's the caterpillar fungus season now, and isn't there a ton of it on his family's land? Maybe he went to the county seat today to sell his caterpillar fungus.* His train of thought having reached this juncture, he looked around and saw absolutely no one, not so much as a bird, on top of which it would be dark soon. All of a sudden his heart began to pound, he felt hot all over, and his whole body became moist with sweat.

And still Orgyen continued with his heartfelt words of advice and admonishment for Dukkar Tsering. From the look of it, he loved and cared for him as he would his own son. And, in fact, wasn't it the old man and other kindhearted neighbors like him who had gotten Dukkar Tsering out from under his debt several times over, selflessly handing over the money earned with their own sweat and toil?

Ah kha, *how could I be so ungrateful to those who've helped me? If I did it, I might get away with it in this life, but certainly not in the next*, thought Dukkar Tsering, calming down, but again his previous thoughts came back to him. *But how can I go back home empty handed like this? How can I show my face to my family? What am I going to give to Grandma?* Once more he looked around and saw that it was almost dark, and the horizon was fading from view. His heart began to pound again and he felt hot all over. His throat became dry and he found it hard to swallow . . .

THREE

At that moment a rabbit bounded out in front of them and tore off into the distance, startling Orgyen's horse, which reared to the side with a snort. The old man, taken by surprise, was tossed from the horse's back like a bird struck by an arrow. Just getting thrown from a horse isn't all that serious, but unfortunately the old man's right foot was caught in the stirrup and he was pulled to the underside of the animal, which startled it even more, and it flailed, reared, and spun around uncontrollably. The old man was tossed between the horse's legs like an empty bag, and as the "bread cakes" in his pocket were thrown in all directions, it became apparent that they were actually wooden nose rings used for cattle. Seen from the edge, their shape and color made them look exactly like bread cakes.

As though he'd suddenly awakened from a terrible nightmare, Dukkar Tsering leaped forward and grabbed the reins, at which point the horse, snorting and quivering, fell still. The old man was groaning as he dangled by the horse's belly, head to the ground and feet to the sky.

Dukkar Tsering held the horse's muzzle fast with his left hand, and with his right removed the old man's foot from the stirrup. Orgyen sat, cradling his head.

Some blood was dripping from Orgyen's nose and mouth, but apart from that he didn't seem to be badly hurt. "Good boy, if it weren't for you I'd be roaming the *bardo* right now," he said after a moment of rest, enunciating every syllable.

"Let's get back to the county seat and take you to a doctor."

"No, I think I'm fine. Here, give me a hand, let's see if I can stand."

Orgyen managed to stand without any difficulty, and as he paced back and forth by himself, he said, "My boy, it's about time for an old man like me to pass on, but as you know, my parents are still alive. There's nothing more terrible than losing your son when you're eighty years old, so I can't go yet. For that reason I will never forget your kindness."

As he gathered up the nose rings that had been tossed all over the place, Dukkar Tsering felt ashamed and terrified of the foolish, fearful notions he'd just had in his head. "That rabbit saved your life. That rabbit saved my life too. That rabbit was a bodhisattva, and no mistake," he blurted.

"What? That harelip rabbit almost killed me!"

". . ."

"Tomorrow I'm going to tell everyone in the camp about how you saved my life, and I'll get them all to help you out again. But you should really give up gambling for real this time."

"If I gamble again, then I'm truly not a man, I'm a dog. Swear on the Three Jewels," Dukkar Tsering vowed both willingly and resolutely.

"Excellent. 'A good man keeps his word and a jackal follows its tracks.'"

"Just you wait and see. I won't need any help this time. I'll pay off my debt through my own hard work."

"That's good. But regardless, I still need to repay you somehow."

Just then, a conchlike full moon appeared in the sky and illuminated the vast landscape as though it were the middle of the day.

Dukkar Tsering helped old Orgyen onto his horse and led it away. The thousand-pound burden that had been weighing him down seemed to disappear without a trace and, filled with happiness, he couldn't help but sing:

Over the mountain peak in the east
the clear white moon rises,
and the face of my beloved
appears in my heart again.

12

BROTHERS

Chökyong Tashi's older brother, Dukkar Tsering, was only forty-five years old, but his hair, short like a monk's, was already ashen gray. His red-rimmed eyes were ashen gray just like his hair, and his swarthy features were covered in wrinkles that looked as though they'd been scribbled on by a naughty child, all of which gave you the impression that he must be a man of at least fifty. When he was thirteen, their father had contracted liver disease and become as thin as a hungry ghost. He'd hung on for the best part of a year, enduring unbearable agony, before finally passing away. As Dukkar Tsering was the oldest of the three siblings, the weight of the entire family's affairs fell on his adolescent shoulders, and it's not hard to imagine just how tough this was for him.

Every time Chökyong Tashi was bullied by other kids, Dukkar Tsering's eyes turned red and his chest heaved with rage, and wiping away Chökyong Tashi's tears, he squeezed him to his chest and led him home. If his brother or sister had a fever or a toothache, Dukkar Tsering took them to the hospital or brought a doctor to see them, day or night, and regardless of the weather. Whenever he went to the county seat he bought a new shirt or a new pair of shoes for his sister, mother, or brother, without ever replacing his own tattered old shirt, causing his mother to shed tears of happiness, or perhaps of sorrow. In his pure, artless mind Chökyong Tashi thought that his brother was the best person in the world and that when he grew up he would repay his kindness. After he did get older and a bit wiser, he heard people say that the hardest thing in the world to repay was a parent's kindness, but as far he was concerned, it wasn't his parents' kindness, but his brother's.

As time went by they all grew older, and Chökyong Tashi's older sister, Rinchen Kyi, married into the Dzongön family, a clan from the lower reaches of the Machu river. Though the Dzongön were historically a branch of the four major clans of Tsezhung, after the Communist Party took power the Dzongön clan fell under the jurisdiction of another province. Nevertheless, their traditional ties continued unbroken in the form of a mutual exchange of brides and grooms.

Not a year after that, Dukkar Tsering himself married a woman from the Dzongön clan. She was a very petite, crimson-cheeked woman, but despite her stature she went about her labors with an inexhaustible supply of strength, and with another, even more inexhaustible supply of strength she dictated her husband's every thought and action. Before long she established a total monopoly of power over the household. She began to treat her mother-in-law as an inanimate object instead of a living thing, forcing the old lady to place all her hopes for care in her twilight years in Chökyong Tashi. "Mama's little darling, get yourself a woman soon, Mama wants to move in with you," she kept saying to him.

A few years later Chökyong Tashi finally got himself a wife and established his own household, but not only did his brother refuse to give him his rightful share of the family land, livestock, and property, he also said that if their mother didn't remain in her own home he'd become the subject of people's gossip.

"Well, how about we just let Mom decide?" This was the first time that Chökyong Tashi had put forward an opinion that conflicted with his brother's.

"What?" spat his brother angrily. "You shameless little shit! Have you forgotten everything I did to raise you?" he yelled, working himself up into a rage.

"No, I haven't, and that's exactly why I said nothing when you didn't give me my fair share of the inheritance."

"Your fair share of the inheritance? Haha! Sounds like you think *you* should be the one living in the old house."

At this point their mother issued a horrible moan. "If neither of you will give me a place to live, then I'll go and live with my daughter." As she prepared to head off to the Dzongön clan, she was accosted by some of her neighbors and the community elders, who urged her to stay at Dukkar Tsering's house. Dukkar Tsering should get his wife under control and take care of his mother, they added, and offered to mediate the dispute.

The tangible outcome of this mediation amounted to nothing more than conferring ownership of their mother's land and livestock on Dukkar Tsering, who did absolutely nothing to get his wife under control, forcing his mother to spend most of her time at Chökyong Tashi's house. Eventually, unable to stand it any longer, she moved to Chökyong Tashi's place for good, "empty hands stuck in her armpits and empty bowl stuck in her pocket," as the saying goes. After that, Chökyong Tashi told his brother that he ought to transfer their mother's share of land over to him, but his brother wouldn't hear of it. "It was you who put Mom up to this and got her to move to your place, giving me a bad name," he said. "Everyone knows your game is to get Mom's share of the land and property all for yourself. But I won't let you take it. Go report me to whoever you like." Chökyong Tashi realized that right from the beginning his brother had been like the man who's thinking not of the yak, but of the meat: what he wanted wasn't his mom, but her land. This must have been the idea of that red-faced wife of his, he thought. He lost all hope for his brother, and the two of them didn't speak for over ten years.

During those years the Dzongön clan began to encroach more and more on the territory of Tsezhung with each passing day and month, flagrantly eating away their grass and wantonly drinking up their water. Both the local authorities and the people of Tsezhung lodged numerous complaints with their Dzongön counterparts, but in the end they responded by claiming that more than a quarter of the present territory of Tsezhung formerly belonged to the Dzongön clan and therefore should be theirs to use. Apparently the population of the farming villages in the lower reaches of the Machu had been expanding rapidly, and they had been muscling their way into the Dzongön's territory as the months and years passed, leaving the Dzongön clan with little choice but to themselves encroach on the land of the Tsezhung clan. So the two sides began to offer large sums of money for the acquisition of rifles. In the autumn of the past year, nine men of the Dzongön clan had been killed, and six had been killed on the Tsezhung side. From that point on, any man or animal that crossed over the mountain pass with the cairn or the other borders that divided the two sides never came back, and guerilla ambushes and the theft of livestock became commonplace.

The pastures belonging to Dukkar Tsering and his brother were both connected to the mountain pass with the cairn, meaning that the last few years hadn't given them enough peace to even enjoy a quiet cup of tea.

As Chökyong Tashi, lugging a rusty 7.9mm rifle that must have been buried under the mountain pass for decades, was grazing his meager, mixed-up herd of sheep and cattle, he saw ten or so yaks running straight toward the pass, tails sticking up over their buttocks. Thinking that he should stop the herd, he mounted his horse and cantered toward them, but when he got there he realized that the yaks were in fact his brother's. He was immediately brought back to the years of terrible treatment he and his mother had endured at the hands of Dukkar Tsering and that wife of his, and he turned his horse back around, feeling the rage build inside him.

Dukkar Tsering was riding a black *dzo*, spurring it on with stirrups and whip in an effort to catch up with his herd, but the yaks were still about a quarter mile away from him and running even faster than before. He looked on helplessly as they disappeared over the tip of the mountain pass with the cairn. Incredibly, Dukkar Tsering, casting his brother an angry glare, continued to ride after his herd without a moment's hesitation. Now Chökyong Tashi looked on helplessly as his brother neared the pass.

Ah ho, *he's really going over the pass, and he's not carrying a gun! His kid probably took that busted rifle to go guard some other bit of land.* Chökyong Tashi felt a sudden wave of alarm and regret. *What am I thinking? My brother's always been so good to me.* With these thoughts running through his mind, he spurred his horse onward.

Just after Dukkar Tsering disappeared over the pass, a gunshot rang out and a prolonged echo filled the air. A flock of wild doves resting on the sunny side of the peak shot into the air, and after circling once, landed back on the shady side of the mountain.

Chökyong Tashi urged on his horse with his spurs and his whip. A succession of images from his childhood appeared before him— his brother guiding him by the hand, lifting him onto his back, kissing him on the head, ruffling his hair, bringing new clothes home for him—and he didn't think to take his rifle from his back, didn't give a thought to the terrible guns on the other side. As soon as he disappeared over the pass, another gunshot rang out and another prolonged echo filled the air. The flock of doves resting on the shady side of the mountain shot into the air, and after circling once, landed back on the sunny side of the peak.

This was an afternoon in the middle of summer. The earth kept on spinning, and the birds and bugs kept on singing and dancing.

A few days later a woman came over the mountain pass with a yak in tow—it was Rinchen Kyi. The yak was loaded on both sides with the putrid corpses of the two brothers, Dukkar Tsering and Chökyong Tashi.

13

THE LAST MAN TO CARE FOR HIS PARENTS

As the photojournalist was hunting for the last remaining wild musk deer on the Qinghai-Tibet plateau, a fierce storm rolled in and drove him to the home of a local nomad named Tsetar Bum, where he took shelter for the night.

A few days later he penned an article entitled "The Last Man to Care for His Parents," which he published in the newspaper and online. In the article he wrote about how Tsetar Bum was an ordinary nomad of Tsezhung County who lived in a ten-yard-square mud hut that he called his "house," which was located in a remote valley sixty miles from the county seat. He was about thirty years old, but he'd never actually been to this county seat. His father was bedridden, and Tsetar Bum had been helping him go to the toilet for over ten years. His mother had been blind for nine years. After his parents became like this, Tsetar Bum's wife took the kids and left. Tsetar Bum had a younger sister and a younger brother, but his sister had long since left to get married and his brother had long since left to become a monk. Tsetar Bum relied on the meager income he received from renting out his land to take care of his invalid parents and to lead an ascetic life of chanting and religious practice, free from any ill will whatsoever.

Shortly thereafter reporters from across the land, extremely dubious of the story, gathered in Tsezhung County like clouds in the autumn. The County Party Committee not only arranged for the head of the Propaganda Department to personally escort the reporters to Tsetar Bum's house, they also had him personally translate for them. The scene was just like a press conference organized for a major affair of state. The press pack jostled with one another and shot their hands in the air, and whoever was given permission by the head of the Propaganda Department directed their question to Tsetar Bum.

Reporter A: "Mr. Tsetar Bum, are you aware that, in the present era, you are probably the only person in the whole world who takes care of his parents?"

"The only person in the whole world? Three Jewels, that's completely impossible."

Reporter B: "Mr. Tsetar Bum, what is your reason for taking care of your parents?"

"*Ah tsi*, what are you talking about? I've never heard of needing a reason to take care of your parents."

Reporter C: "Mr. Tsetar Bum, it is my understanding that you also have a sister and a brother. If that's true, wouldn't it be better for the three of you to at least take turns looking after your parents?"

"Take turns? I've never heard of such a thing. If you have the chance to take care of your parents, it's your good fortune for accumulating merit. Besides, my sister left to get married ages ago, so she belongs to another family now. My brother's taken his vows and wears the robes of a monk. How could I possibly expect him to wipe someone's butt?"

Reporter D: "Mr. Tsetar Bum, in that case, do your sister and brother provide you with any support?"

"Of course they do. My sister makes me *tsampa* and brings me butter and cheese and yogurt and milk. And my brother buys me salt and tea."

Reporter E: "Mr. Tsetar Bum, it is my understanding that your county seat has an old people's home. Why don't you send your parents there? That way you could get married, have kids, have a happy life."

"These people's questions are so strange. Why would a son send his parents to an old people's home if he's still alive? Heh, if I get married and have a kid, and he sends me to an old folks' home when I get old, isn't that just so he can have a happy life himself?"

Reporter F: "Mr. Tsetar Bum, I have a rather impolite question. Does your brain work normally? Have you ever been to see a doctor? My apologies."

"Heh, if it's true that I'm the only person in the whole world who takes care of his parents . . . heh, then I think my brain works more normally than anyone's."

Reporter G: "Mr. Tsetar Bum, it is my understanding that you haven't been outside of this place once in twenty or thirty years, and that you've never even been to the county seat. There have been enormous changes in the outside world in the last thirty years; don't you want to go and see what it's like?"

"Heh, sounds like one of those changes is that I've become the only one who takes care of his parents. Three Jewels, I couldn't stomach seeing changes like that."

The reporters fell silent. In their minds this scruffy nomad had gradually transformed into some sort of dazzling international dignitary. For a moment they became overawed, and no one dared ask another question.

Plucking up his courage, the final reporter asked, "Are your actions the fruits of Tsezhung County's long propaganda campaign to promote Spiritual Civilization?"

"I don't understand this question," Tsetar Bum said to the head of the Propaganda Department.

"He said, 'That goes without saying,'" the head of the Propaganda Department translated for the reporters.

Following a vigorous publicity drive by the reporters and a concerted campaign of self-aggrandizement by the Propaganda Department, Tsezhung County was awarded the title of Nation-wide Leading County in Spiritual Civilization.

14

BLACK FOX VALLEY

ONE

About forty miles north of the Tsezhung county seat was a mountain pass with a small cairn and a few strings of prayer flags. If you looked out from the pass, you would see a valley opening to the north covered in a rich variety of dense thickets. In the middle of the valley, in a marsh about the size of a sheep pen, gushing springs were dotted all around, their waters merging and forming a clear stream that flowed down through the center of the vale. In July and August, its deep reaches became a dense wilderness of shrubs—spiraea, black and white dasiphora, rhododendrons—each with a variety of flowers blooming atop them. Up on the ridges, edelweiss and stellera grew by the bunch, and gentians bloomed in the autumn. Both banks of the stream in the middle of the valley were covered in wolfsbane, lousewort and long tube lousewort, maroon snow lotus, and all sorts of other flowers. On the smooth grasslands down at the foot of the valley grew leopard plants, knotweed, lamiophlomis, white snow lotus, black and white gentians, Himalayan aster, Tibetan dandelions, white wormwood, potentilla, and countless other things that even someone who could boast of being an expert in botany would be hard pressed to identify. Every few days, the hues of the landscape transformed and a new variety of fragrances filled the air. If the "Thousand Lotus Pasture" described in the *Epic of Gesar* really exists, then it must be this very place.

If you laid your eyes on the scene of the nomads' dwelling here—the air peppered with the occasional sounds of five or six hundred whinnying horses, lowing cattle, and bleating sheep, living peacefully and carefree—that phrase "exquisite pastures richly endowed" would naturally come to mind.

This valley had something of an unusual name: Black Fox Valley. This wasn't just because the foxes there were black—even the marmots were. No one in Tsezhung had ever really paid any attention to this, but when Sangyé's family was given a pasturage contract for use of the valley, Sangyé began to consider the matter seriously. *This doesn't bode well. Foxes everywhere else are red. Why is it that only the foxes in this valley are black?* he wondered, plucking his moustache. Once, when the people of Tsezhung had invited Alak Drong to visit the community, Sangyé came to kneel before him and seek his counsel. "Venerable Rinpoché, foxes everywhere else are red. Only the foxes in my family's pasture are black, and so the valley's called Black Fox Valley. Do you think we need to do a prayer service or something?" The reason he said "my family's pasture" was that some county and township officials had carried out a cartographic survey and, after making some marks on the map, had given him a booklet called a "Pasture Usage Permit." In this book was written, in both Chinese and Tibetan, the acreage of the pasture, its boundaries, and that it had been allocated to Sangyé's family for a period of fifty years.

Alak Drong handed Sangyé a piece of paper on which was written two lines of cursive script.

Sangyé took the paper, and along with one hundred yuan, handed it to a monk he knew at Tsezhung Monastery.

TWO

Sangyé was fifty years old and thin, and had a swarthy complexion. His jaw was covered all over in scattered whiskers of unequal lengths. Some years ago he had possessed a pair of tweezers with a bat design on it, and his facial hair hadn't been as abundant then as it was now. Unfortunately, however, either Sangyé, his wife, Ludrön, or one of their kids had accidentally trod or knelt on the tweezers, bending them out of shape and compromising their hair-plucking capacity. Even more unfortunately, one time when the family was moving camp the tweezers simply disappeared. Ever since then his facial hair had continued to grow longer and thicker. There was nothing else he could do. As soon as he found himself with idle hands he'd seize the opportunity, and with his left hand plying his prayer beads, his right would work at the moustache, plucking hairs between the nails of his thumb and index finger. This was especially the case when he was thinking or when he was worried—in the blink of an eye he'd be plucking his moustache. Sadly, his fingernails were far less effective than those tweezers.

Sangyé was normally a very quiet and gentle man, but he actually had a sharp tongue. Before he got his pasturage contract, he and the other guys from the community would get together just to brag and banter. Once, Gönpo Tashi, a big tubby guy with a dark complexion, had said to him, "Ya—skinny Sangyé the makpa,[1] Akhu Jamyang's family has got you tanned as soft as sheepskin. Won't even let you eat your fill! How will you last through the spring? You poor thing!" Everyone burst out laughing.

Sangyé responded, "Ya—fatty Gönpo. You ate your own portion and then everyone else's, now you've got a belly as big as a

---

1. A man who marries and moves in with his wife's family.

yak's and you can barely stand upright. If only that yak's belly was on the butcher's block—one little cut of the knife and you'd see yellow fat for sure. It's just a shame the smell would be so bad not even a dog would eat it, never mind a man." Everyone burst out laughing again.

Gönpo Tashi was on the verge of offering a rebuttal, but Sangyé didn't give him the chance. "*Ya*, fatty Gönpo, you been serenading your sister recently?" Everyone laughed even harder than before. Gönpo Tashi, realizing that he was no match for Sangyé, gave a chuckle. "All right, all right. You win for today."

"Serenading your sister" was a reference to an embarrassing episode for Gönpo Tashi. Not long after he got married, Gönpo Tashi was coming back from the county seat when he saw a girl riding a yak up ahead of him. Following behind, he serenaded her with a string of love songs, informing her of his bachelor status and inquiring as to whether or not she had a lover, and if not, whether she we would like to form a romantic bond. The terrified woman spurred on her yak and tried to escape as fast as she could, but how could a yak possibly compete with a horse? In a flash he caught up with her, only to discover that this was none other than his little sister, who some time before had gotten married and moved to another community. With his face burning with shame and no idea what to do, he spun his horse around and galloped off.

On any given day Sangyé's wife, Ludrön, would talk nonstop until she fell asleep: the son of the local branch secretary had gone off to become a monk, the village head had bought a little car, the money that new family got for their fifty sheep was all counterfeit, we need to make a new winter coat for Mom this year, we need to decide whether we're going to marry our daughter to that harelip Mikyang, okay? She would go on and on like this, and today was no exception.

"Give it a bloody rest, will you? Even if your mouth's not hurting, my ears are."

"When you've got a mouth you've got a right to use it. If your ears hurt, then just don't listen."

Sangyé didn't want to argue with her, so he plucked his moustache and fell silent. Ludrön continued, "When we got our pasturage contract, didn't they say it was for fifty years? Now they're saying, 'Return the Pastures to Restore the Grasslands.' What's all that about? If we move to one of those compounds, then where's the meat, butter, and cheese going to come from? Akhu Sönam's family said they've decided not to move to the county seat."

Sangyé became even more annoyed. "What's the point in bringing all this up now, eh? We've already sold some of the livestock, and we've paid our share, the zee-chow. The government's already built the house, and most of the families have moved to the town. And another thing—we just need to leave the pastures fallow for a few years, then the deeds will return to the nomads. If there comes a day when we really can't get by, then we'll come back. When your mom and dad get back from Lhasa, we're moving to the town."

"What? I thought we were moving after the new year."

"Most of the families have already moved to the county seat, so there won't be anyone here for the new year anyway. Besides, I heard the houses there are great. Wouldn't it be nicer to spend the new year in a new house?"

". . ."

Ludrön's father, Jamyang, was seventy-two, and her mother, Yangdzom, was seventy. Though neither of them had completely lost the ability to work, all the authority in the family had long since been passed on to the son-in-law, Sangyé. For that reason, most of the people in the community didn't call them the "Jamyang family," but the "Sangyé family." Sangyé's son Lhagön Kyab had been sent off to school, and after finishing primary school he went to Labrang Monastery to become a monk, where he took the name Gendün Gyatso. A few days previously he had taken his grandparents, his older sister, Lhatso Kyi, and her daughter to Lhasa on a pilgrimage.

Sangyé no longer had a single thing he needed to take care of, but this made him feel even more unsettled than before. He plucked his moustache vigorously.

THREE

One freezing cold morning, Sangyé hired two of the small hand tractors that the nomads called a "show-foo." In one he piled up sacks of dung, on top of which he laid a whole yak carcass, a bag of butter, and other assorted provisions. Then came the tent, bound up in a rectangular bundle; fur-lined coats and mattresses; pans, bowls, and other clothes and utensils. In the other tractor he laid down more sacks of dung, and on top he placed the altar, his family, and the dog. Amid the relentless chugging sound and the black smoke emitted by the engine, they set off on the smooth main road that led from the mountain pass of Black Fox Valley. Instinctively, the whole family turned as one to look back at the valley where their little adobe house lay. Just when they reached the mountain pass, Sangyé pulled a pack of prayer flags from his pocket and tossed them into the air, yelling "Victory to the gods!" as loudly as he could. Just at that moment, the driver pushed the tractor to full throttle, drowning out his cry.

At around three o'clock they finally arrived at the Tsezhung county seat. Here, there was one phrase that they absolutely had to remember: *Xingfu Shengtai Yimin Cun* (the Chinese for Happy Ecological Resettlement Village). When they stopped to ask someone for directions, telling him that they were one of those families that had Returned the Pastures to Restore the Grasslands and come to the county seat, his response was, "You need to go to the *shengtai yimin cun*. But there are lots of *shengtai yimin cuns*. Whereabouts are you from?"

"We're from Tsezhung."

"Tsezhung, Tsezhung . . . I think most of the *yimin* from Tsez-hung are on the north side of town. Anyway, just ask where *Xingfu Shengtai Yimin Cun* is and you'll be fine."

"What?" Sangyé plucked his moustache incessantly. "Shampoo sheng . . ."

"*Xingfu Shengtai Yimin Cun.*"

At that point the tractor drivers interjected, telling Sangyé they had to get off. If the family wanted to keep on looking for the place, they said, then an additional fee would be required.

"How much?"

"Ten yuan for each *shoufu*, and we'll take you to *Xingfu Shengtai Yimin Cun.*"

"All right, we'll do that."

The moment the tractor did a U-turn, a traffic cop appeared and signaled for them to stop. The two drivers instantly turned pale. In the same moment, they hit the brakes and set their feet on the ground, ready to make themselves scarce. But the police-man, paying no attention to them, was looking transfixed at the tractor. "You selling antiques? Bronze pots, copper kettles, Bud-dha statues, *thangka* paintings, old rugs, used flints, teacups or hair ornaments from a dead relative, that sort of thing? Anyway, the older, the better."

"We've got a saddle . . ." began Ludrön, but before she could continue Sangyé cut her off. "Where is the shampoo sheng tai . . . house?"

The policeman didn't understand a word Sangyé was saying. He turned back to Ludrön: "You're selling a saddle? Does it have a metal inlay? Is it antique?"

"It's that one." Ludrön pointed to Sangyé's inlaid saddle, which was sitting on the other tractor. "We don't have a horse anymore, what are we going to do with a saddle? If someone wants to buy it, we might as well sell it. It's just getting in the way."

The policeman looked closely at the saddle. "I'll give you five thousand."

"We're not selling the saddle."

Suddenly, the policeman's eyes turned to the family guard dog. "How much for the dog?"

"We're not selling the dog, absolutely no way!" the whole family cried, virtually in unison. "Shampoo sheng tai ..." began Sangyé again. The policeman ignored him. He was ignoring the two drivers as well, so they started up the tractors and took off.

After about a mile the tractors came to a stop. "This is *Xingfu Shengtai Yimun Cun*. Get off, pay up."

FOUR

Seen from a distance, the countless rows of neatly arranged houses, identical in size and color, looked just like bricks laid out to dry in a brickyard. Each house was also enclosed by walls that were, likewise, identical to one another in color and size. At the main gate of the compound, there was a large sign written in Chinese: *Xingfu Shengtai Yimin Cun*. If you were looking for a family who lived here, it would be no good at all to adopt that backward old bumpkin method where you just say, "Hey buddy! Where's the Sangyé family from Tsezhung?" It was absolutely imperative to know the house number of the Sangyé family. For instance, if this Sangyé family lived at compound 21, row 17, unit 4, then you had to look for house number 211704. For an illiterate nomad, this was by no means an easy feat, but today the family was accompanied by Gendün Gyatso, their son who had left to become a monk. Even more fortunately, they bumped into someone from their community who had moved there about ten days ago. He took Sangyé to see an official who had hair as red as blood, a face as cold as winter, and hands as slow as a tortoise. Without much trouble at all they soon obtained a big bunch of keys and a slip of paper bearing their house number.

Each family got a three-room house, in front of which was a little enclosure called a "garden." Iron sheets and tubing constituted the main door, above which was planted a red flag with five yellow stars; they were told that anytime it got dirty or worn out it could be replaced for free. The walls were made of whitewashed hollow cement bricks, upon which was painted a crimson border dotted with white decorations. The minute that Sangyé's family saw these houses—so replete with ethnic characteristics—they felt a warm glow in their hearts. Jamyang was especially moved. "The kindness of the Party! How can we ever repay it?" he uttered hoarsely, tears welling at the corners of his eyes as he surveyed the houses. "Not even Alak Drong's mansion is better than this! What have we done to deserve such good fortune?"

One of the rooms of the house was divided in two by a partition wall. One half appeared to be the kitchen, and the other must have been the bathroom, as a big toilet made of white porcelain had been installed in the corner. Sangyé and his wife thought at first that this was some kind of wash basin, causing Gendün Gyatso to snort with derision. "It's for doing your number ones and twos."

"What?" cried Grandpa Jamyang. "Pissing and crapping in a lovely basin like this? We'd use up so much merit our assholes would close up!" Yangdzom agreed. "If we don't know what it is, let's leave it be. Anyway, you're having a laugh if you say that's for number ones and twos."

"*Ah tsi!* I swear on the Three Jewels, it's for taking a crap in," Gendün Gyatso insisted. "Toilets like this are everywhere these days. I've used them loads of times." As it so happened, he was struck at that very moment by the irrepressible urge do his business. Hoisting up his robe, he planted himself on the toilet and was overcome with a great wave of relief as he dropped an enormous load. Much to his surprise, however, no matter how much he flushed, not a drop of water appeared in the bowl. When he took a closer look, he discovered that there was no pipe connected to the toilet. So it was left to his sister, Lhatso Kyi, to cover her nose and mouth with her left hand, and with her right dispose of the foul mess in the toilet.

Though the house had a toilet, it had no stove, so Sangyé had to go into town to buy one. He picked up a plastic bottle of milk while he was there, then hired one of the three-wheeled pedicabs they called a "three-legs" to get back home. By the time Ludrön went out to make an offering to the deities it was already almost dusk. The dog barked forlornly from the post in the corner of the yard where he was tied up, and only then did she realize he hadn't eaten anything all day. Overcome by pity for the poor thing, she rushed back inside and grabbed a half pound of boiled blood sausage, which she brought straight back out and gave to the dog. Apart from the fact that he couldn't speak and lived outside, the dog was just like one of the family, and he'd stuck to them like a shadow for six or seven years. How unexpected, then, that this was to be his last meal at home with them. The next day, they awoke to discover that the dog, along with his leash, had vanished as if he'd been swallowed up by the ground. The whole family was devastated, their only consolation being that at least he hadn't left on an empty stomach.

FIVE

Nomads call dogs that steal food "thieving dogs," and, in the same way, shameless thieves are also called "thieving dogs." But it's the thieves who steal dogs who are really and truly the shameless "thieving dogs." Sangyé, plucking at his moustache, was preoccupied with the question of who these thieving dogs could be, as well as the matter of all the household appliances that needed to be bought: a television, a fridge, a bed, a thermos, curtains, and other things besides.

The Western new year had passed, and the Tibetan new year was approaching. Officials from the county and township authorities arrived, bringing the financial subsidies for the Return the Pastures to Restore the Grasslands program as well as a bounty of flour, rice, oil, tea, multicolored calendars, and other odds and ends to mark the "Two New Years" or "Two Festivals." They also asked people if they had any problems or needs—just let them know, they said, and it would be sorted out right away. Sangyé's family was deeply moved, Jamyang and Yangdzom especially so. "The great kindness of the Party! The great kindness of the nation!" Jamyang declared, unable to hold back the tears. "We didn't lift a finger and they give us all this money and all these things! Is this a dream? Praise be! Such kindness! Such kindness! We have no problems or needs, none at all." He was virtually prostrating himself. After the officials had left, Jamyang eagerly drummed into the whole family—Sangyé and his son especially—the lesson to never forget the benevolence of the Communist Party, to always keep it in mind, whether in tent or temple. "When you go into town," he added, "buy a portrait of the leader." By "the leader" Jamyang meant Mao Zedong, but when Sangyé went to the Xinhua bookstore, he not only bought portraits of Mao Zedong, Deng Xiaoping, Jiang Zemin, and Hu Jintao, he also got a portrait of Stalin, faded from its many years of lying there without a buyer. He stuck them above the altar, a space already filled with all manner of different-sized pictures of Alak Drong and other lamas and *trülkus*, and it seemed that a new splendor and radiance had been added to their home. When Jamyang turned his prayer wheel or Sangyé idly plucked his moustache, each would turn involuntarily toward the portraits of the leaders and gaze upon them with awe and reverence.

Getting food on the table and clothes on their backs without having to do a bit of work for it—this was something they couldn't have even dreamed of before. And so it seemed that Happy Ecological Resettlement Village was indeed a happy place. But, a short while later, Jamyang got it into his head that he should take a trip into town and ask around about their missing dog while he was there. Many years ago, he had been a grassroots-level cadre and had often gone to town to take part in "Three-Grade Conferences" and the like. In those days, he knew this little town like the back of his hand, but now, with development surging at the pace of a galloping horse, the place had changed beyond recognition. He wasn't at all confident he'd be able to find his way back to Happy Ecological Resettlement Village, and even if he could, there was no way he'd be able to remember that house number—which might as well have been written in hieroglyphics—so he lost his nerve. Now, deprived of the ability to go out, he began to feel like a prisoner in his own home. He spent every day sitting despondently in the doorway, his view curtailed by the rows and rows of houses blocking the horizon. Once, as he was staring at the corner of the yard where the dog used to be, the image of Black Fox Valley appeared before his eyes and the sound of barking rang distantly in his ears. From then on, Jamyang spoke less and less with each passing day.

Sangyé bought a color TV, a fridge, and a sofa. Now the family was able to watch TV shows in Tibetan, which brought a new joy to their lives. Most popular of all was the "New Year Special" they saw on New Year's Eve, a kind of variety show that completely captivated their attention. And now they could finally lay their eyes on the comedian Menla Kyab, whom they used to talk about like he was Old Man Earth himself.

There were two major events at New Year. The first was that their daughter, Lhatso Kyi, was married to Mikyang the harelip. The other was that, in keeping with Yangdzom's wishes, Lhari Kyi,

Lhatso Kyi's daughter from a previous relationship, would stay with her mother's family (that is, Sangyé's family) instead of moving in with the new husband. This was on the condition that she would be sent to school when the new term began in the autumn.

SIX

Spring arrived. All at once, men and women in what seemed like their thousands descended upon the Tsezhung county seat. They had come to do all manner of jobs: digging for caterpillar fungus, building houses, constructing highways. In the blink of an eye the grasslands, normally as still as yogurt, began to seethe like boiling water.

The meat, butter, cheese, and dung that Sangyé's family had brought from Black Fox Valley had gradually been used up. Now Sangyé and Ludrön had to take turns going to town for supplies almost every day, and what's more the price of food went up with each trip. As Sangyé was also looking for a job in town, a mile's journey away, getting a motorbike became an urgent necessity. Nomads, who love to exaggerate, have a saying about thieves: "As soon as you bend over, they'll steal your balls." In reality, though, what thieves really like isn't balls, but bikes. If you didn't want to offer up your motorbike to the thieves, then you pretty much had to keep it locked up in the house day and night. The three-room house, which at first had seemed huge and spacious, was now filled not only with their previous belongings but also with all the new things they'd bought since moving in, making the place incredibly cramped. Sangyé was left with no choice but to remove that big toilet, which was no use whatsoever, and put it outside.

"My god!" When the red-haired cadre who had given Sangyé his keys and house number arrived, she cried out in horror. "They've thrown the bloody *matong* outside! My god ... and the *shicha* is coming tomorrow. My god ... what a disaster, an absolute disaster! These people will be the death of me!" She paced back and forth, having no clue what to do.

Sangyé was petrified. He stood rooted to the spot with his mouth hanging open. "It's just taking up space, it's completely useless . . ." said Ludrön.

"Even if it's useless, we still need to show it to the *shicha* when he comes! My god . . . this is no good. I'm done for!"

Ludrön was about to continue when Sangyé cried out, "Oh dear, oh dear, what on earth are we going to do?" He looked at the red-haired woman imploringly, as though hoping to take holy refuge with her.

"Do your dad's head! Go and fetch a *gongren* to reinstall it, quick. If the *shicha* sees this I'm done for."

"A *gongren*?"

"Yes, yes! Get a workman. And quick!"

Sangyé jumped right on his bike and headed for town. Without even asking the price he handed over one hundred yuan and got someone to come back with him. This man mixed one handful of cement with a couple of sand and reinstalled the toilet. When Sangyé thought about the red-haired woman's expression, he felt that the imminent arrival of the so-called "*shicha*" must be a truly terrifying thing. Filled with anxiety, he plucked his moustache ceaselessly and paced back and forth from the house to the gate.

Though the wind had grown so fierce you could hardly open your eyes, Jamyang still spent the whole day sitting on the doorstep spinning his prayer wheel. He stared into the corner of the yard where the dog used to be, growing more and more silent by the day. Sometimes Yangdzom would plop herself in front of him, raising a cloud of dust, and say a couple of words. But apart from a few monosyllabic responses, he paid little attention to her. She could do nothing but sit for a while, then hoist herself up in another cloud of dust, go back inside, and keep watching TV. She didn't care whether the show was in Chinese or Tibetan, just so long as there was something to look at. She didn't really understand the formal Tibetan they spoke on television either, but she still loved to watch. For her, at least, it was easier to get through the days than it was for Jamyang.

Sangyé was still worried about this *"shicha."* Finally, accompanied by a flock of county and township officials, cameramen, and photographers, he arrived. But he was not at all as terrifying as Sangyé had imagined; on the contrary, he was a kind and gentle man, round-bellied and wreathed in smiles just like those Chinese statues of the Buddha you always see. No matter what was said to him, he would respond with a "Ha ha ha! *Hao hao hao!* Good good good!" Even when he took a cursory glance at the useless toilet, the toilet that served no purpose whatsoever but taking up space, his reaction was nothing but a *"Hao hao!"* Only then did Sangyé calm down.

After the kind and gentle *shicha* and his entourage had left, all the other families eventually removed their toilets and dumped them outside, but this time the red-haired woman didn't seem to care. After a few days had passed, Sangyé too plucked up his courage and once again dumped the toilet back outside.

SEVEN

After two months of continuous gales there came the sleet, which gradually became an endless downpour. So much water leaked from the roofs of the houses in Happy Ecological Resettlement Village that they became unlivable. Even worse, as the water flowed down all four walls, outside and in, the residents discovered that the hollow bricks had been stuck together not with cement but with clay. Black muddy water stripped off all the whitewash, leaving the houses completely naked, and cracks began to appear all over the bricks. This posed a serious threat to the portraits of the Party leaders stuck on the wall, and Sangyé was forced to take them down.

"We saved up all this zee-chow money for a house like this? And I heard the government's subsidy was even more than what we paid," fumed Ludrön. "The adobe houses in Black Fox Valley were ugly, but they never leaked. And they were warm too. Mom and Dad are going to freeze to death in this place!" All of a sudden, she was struck by an idea. "Hey, why don't we pitch the tent in the yard and put a stove in there?"

"We . . . I suppose we could do that. But . . ." Sangyé plucked his moustache. "But what will the red-haired woman say?"

"Listen to yourself. You make it sound like she's our boss! She damn well should have something to say if she comes to see this place. It's unbelievable, paying all that zee-chow money for a house like this!"

"I swear on the sutras . . . I'm terrified of that red-haired woman."

"What's there to be afraid of? If you're scared, then I'll go." Ludrön got up and went straight out the door. In truth, she didn't really know if she had the courage to confront the red-haired woman, but having so fearlessly declared to her husband that she would, she was left with no choice. Fortunately, when she got to the red-haired woman's office, the Tsezhung township secretary and other officials, along with a big crowd of nomads, were already gathered there. One of the officials who knew Tibetan was telling them that they'd already sent a report up to the county Party committee and the county government, and that the county Party committee and the county government were taking this matter very seriously indeed, and that when this bad weather had passed they would absolutely fix every single one of the houses. He entreated the broad masses to have patience in this matter.

"In that case, there's nothing more to say. Praise be to the Party and the nation," said a young man with a hoarse voice, seemingly on behalf of the assembled group. He walked out the door, followed in succession by the others.

Ludrön returned home with a smile on her face and reported to the family. "The leaders said to be patient for a few days and they'll fix the house as soon as they can."

"The Party and the nation truly are like our mother and father!" Jamyang, who had been silent for some time now, finally opened his mouth to speak, his face a picture of joy. Sangyé stopped plucking his moustache and said, "I'll go the county seat and get some mutton. This town, it's really amazing. They sell lovely fatty mutton, even in spring!"

The heavy rain finally stopped. On every house, about five inches of moss had sprouted haphazardly at the feet of the sun-facing walls. Repair work began on the houses of the Ecological Resettlement Villages surrounding the Tsezhung county seat, which were now even larger and more numerous than before. The method of repairing the houses was extremely simple: they removed the tiles from the roof, laid down a few plastic sheets, spread about half an inch of black soil on top, then replaced the tiles. After that they coated the walls in a layer of cement about the thickness of the back of a knife, slapped on some whitewash, quickly repainted the vermillion and white decorations, and that was that. Finally, a group of *shicha* who said they were from the prefecture arrived, pronounced it "Very good," and left. Apparently it was indeed very good. For a while after that not a drop of water leaked in, no matter how heavily it rained. But, much to everyone's surprise, when the spring rains came the next year, the very same thing happened again.

Once more, the nomads gathered at the red-haired woman's office. Some demanded the return of their down payments and said that they were going back to the grasslands.

The county Party committee and the county government were taking this matter very seriously indeed. They said that they would repair all of the houses for free. Sadly, their method of repairing the houses was precisely the same as the one they had used the year before. The nomads called this method "spreading mud on shit."

EIGHT

In the Tsezhung county seat, dung sellers were becoming more and more rare, but sellers of another kind of fuel were becoming more and more common. This fuel was coal, a substance that in the past had been the exclusive privilege of the Tsezhung county seat's high officials and wealthy work units. The price of coal was so high that the nomads referred to it as the "expensive black rock." Not only was it expensive, it was also dangerous. In Happy Ecological Resettlement Village alone, nine people from three different families had died of carbon monoxide poisoning. Once, four cadres from the county seat were drinking beer together and passed out in a drunken haze. One of them woke up thirsty in the middle of the night and staggered to the stove to grab the kettle, but he didn't put it back properly, leaving the door of the stove open. In the morning, all four were found dead. Tales such as this were a constant source of terror for the residents of Happy Ecological Resettlement Village. By the grace of the Three Jewels, no such tragedy had befallen Sangyé's family. Still, they were running out of money fast, and on top of that, about a third of the expensive black rock they'd bought recently had turned out to be nonflammable rocks and pebbles. As Sangyé fell deep into thought and plucked his moustache, Ludrön said, "The butter you bought the other day had completely gone off. Yesterday Dad ate some *tsampa* with butter in it, and he said he had a stomachache the whole day. This morning he had to eat plain black *tsampa*. You didn't even check if it was fresh . . ."

"Didn't check if it was fresh?" Sangyé interrupted her. "Fresh butter's as expensive as the heavens!" He plucked his moustache irritably.

"I think it's time to sell the saddle. What's the point of having a saddle when you haven't got a horse?"

"Don't you know the saying 'The horse is easy come, the saddle's hard won'?"

"Well, what about 'If you're blessed with the horse, the saddle's easy to source'?"

"Maybe it's easy to get an ordinary saddle, but mine's no ordinary saddle."

"Well anyway, if we can't get any fresh butter, it's going to be tough for us, let alone Mom and Dad."

"Doesn't matter how tough it is. Without the pasture compensation money, there's nothing I can do."

"Tea with no milk, rancid butter—the poor old things."

"Let me go buy some milk." Who knows if Sangyé felt sorry for the old folks or was just tired of Ludrön's grumbling. Either way, as he got to the door, he saw his son Gendün Gyatso enter the yard.

It seemed as though Gendün Gyatso grasped the whole situation just from seeing his parents' faces. He greeted his grandparents and gave them each a kiss, and without even sitting down he pulled two thousand yuan from his pocket and placed it in his father's hands.

A lot of monks and nuns nowadays are returning to lay life, and when they do, many of the young men gamble and steal, while many of the young women turn to prostitution. In Happy Ecological Resettlement Village alone, five or six men had been arrested and three or four women had disappeared just in the last two years. Not only had four or five monks returned to lay life, one of them actually went back to his monastery and stole a precious black *thangka* of Pelden Lhamo that was even older than the monastery itself. He got caught as he was preparing to make his getaway and was still in jail. Various shocking events such as this had occurred, and they continued to occur. But Gendün Gyatso dedicated himself solely to prayer and the cultivation of merit. He declined the extravagant lifestyle led by other monks, instead saving up all the alms donated by the faithful and using them to help his family. When he thought of all this, Sangyé wanted to squeeze Gendün Gyatso to his chest and kiss him. But not having kissed his son once since he'd grown up, he felt it would be awkward to do it now. Feeling so moved that he might cry, Sangyé excused himself by saying that he was going to buy some meat.

Ludrön followed him out the door, shouting, "Don't forget to buy a bottle of milk! But don't get it from the store by the gung-shang-joo, it's all fake!" This fake milk came in all varieties; the most common was the kind that had been mixed with water and skimmed, as well as the kind that was yak milk passed off as cow milk. There was one kind even demons couldn't think up: during the hot summer months, people would put antibiotics in the milk to stop it from turning.

Sangyé, revving the engine of his bike, didn't seem to hear her. In any case, he didn't respond. "He's going to get fake milk again," Ludrön mumbled to herself as she turned to go back inside. She saw her father, Jamyang, staring at the corner where the dog used to be, and tugged at his sleeve. "Dad, let's go inside."

NINE

As soon as Jamyang entered the house, Gendün Gyatso rose to greet him. Jamyang cast an eye over his grandson and asked, "Who is this monk?"

Gendün Gyatso, completely taken aback, looked over at Ludrön. "Grandpa's confused," she whispered. At that point,

Yangdzom intervened. "*Ah tsi*, what's the matter with this old man? It's your grandson, the monk! He came to say hello to you just now, remember?" But Jamyang didn't accept this at all; in fact, he grew angry. "*Ah tsi*, when did our little monk get here? Why didn't you come say hello to your grandpa?" Gendün Gyatso, not knowing whether to laugh or cry, could only put his arms around his grandpa and give him a kiss. Only then did Jamyang, seemingly satisfied, sit down on the floor.

"Your grandpa's confused," Ludrön whispered again. "Every evening he stands in the doorway saying things like 'Have you fed the dog?' 'Is the old brown *dzo* back in her pen?' 'Tie up the old gray horse with the black one that always bends its head.' I don't even remember us having any animals like that. I asked your grandma, and she said that the old brown *dzo*, the old gray horse, and the black one that always bends its head were all animals they had when they were young. . . ." Her words were flowing like water, but she was brought to a halt when little Lhari Kyi flung open the door and rushed in, panting. "Is Uncle here?"

Before Gendün Gyatso could say anything, Ludrön cut in. "*Ah tsi*, what are you doing home from school so early?"

Lhari Kyi put down her backpack, and in a mix of Tibetan and Chinese announced two unrelated items of news. The first was that the roof of one of the classrooms had caved in, crushing two children to death and injuring four more. The second was that yesterday a student had gone into one of the teacher's houses and stolen some money, and the teacher had beaten him black and blue. So today the kid's older brother had gotten some of his friends together, and they'd beaten the teacher until he couldn't stand.

"The *xiaozhang* said we didn't have to *shang ke* today," said Lhari Kyi, concisely concluding her explanation of why they were released from school early.

"*Ah ho!* What if our little baby had been crushed . . . that's it, no more school from now on!" said Yangdzom with an iron resolve, squeezing Lhari Kyi tightly to her breast. Of all the members of the family, she was most attached to Lhari Kyi. When Lhatso Kyi had married into another family, Yangdzom had been absolutely insistent that the child not be taken away, and she'd also been reluctant to send her off to school. For this reason she now seized the opportunity before her in the hope that that she could keep Lhari Kyi by her side day and night.

They heard the sound of a motorbike pulling up outside. Not long after, Sangyé entered, followed by a middle-aged woman carrying a heavy saddlebag on her left shoulder; it was Yudrön, Sangyé's younger sister. The region in which Yudrön lived hadn't yet undergone "ecological resettlement." Not only did her family not have to buy livestock products, they'd actually been able to sell some, and Yudrön, with great generosity, had even given some things away for free. It was for this reason that, every time she came to the county seat, she brought meat, butter, cheese, milk, yogurt, and other things besides for her brother's family. This time too, she came bearing a whole rump of mutton, four pounds of wrapped-up yak offal, an eleven-pound block of butter, seven pounds of cheese in a black plastic bag, a plastic tub of yogurt, and two plastic bottles of milk. On top of all that, as she greeted Jamyang, Yangdzom, and Lhari Kyi, she gave each of them ten yuan.

Sangyé had also bought a few plastic bottles of the sugary soda they called "kow-lah" and seven pounds of yak meat. Ludrön set straight to chopping meat and kneading dough for dumplings. She put a generous heap of coal in the stove, and soon it was burning with a red flame that filled the room with warmth. They began to chat about this and that, and the sound of laughter, which had become a rarity, rang intermittently through the house. The troubles that had so burdened Sangyé and Ludrön only a few hours before, as well as the terrible things Lhari Kyi had told them about the school, were all seemingly forgotten. Jamyang was the first to turn in, followed shortly by Yangdzom with Lhari Kyi asleep in her arms. The others all stayed up for a good two hours past their normal bedtimes.

At the end of this joy-filled day, Sangyé went outside to relieve himself one last time, but was greeted by an unpleasant surprise. "*Ah ho! Ah ho!* My mow-tow! My mow-tow! Those thieving dogs, the thieving dogs . . ." he cried, pacing around the yard hopelessly looking for his missing motorbike.

TEN

The red-haired woman—as she was secretly referred to by the inhabitants of Happy Ecological Resettlement Village—came to Sangyé's house to demand immediate payment of the electricity and water bills. If they didn't pay, she told them, the electricity would be cut off and they wouldn't be allowed to draw water.

Sangyé had grown in confidence of late, and his mood had also turned darker. Without a hint of fear, he responded, "When you pay me the pastures subsidy, I'll pay the bills. Otherwise you can go ahead and cut off the electricity. I'll use a solar generator. And if I'm not allowed to draw water, then we'll just get it from the Tsechu River."

The red-haired woman laughed. "Haha! Everyone knows the Tsechu is so *wuran*-ed that not even pigs will drink from it."

Sangyé was about to retort when Ludrön unleashed a shrill, heart-rending cry and dashed forward three or four paces. She turned around, mouth agape, as though her spirit had left her body.

Sangyé swung around and saw Jamyang collapsed face down on the ground. He leaped forward and lifted Jamyang's head, but the old man's body had already turned cold.

According to Ludrön, her father had been sitting straight as a rod, and when she tugged at his sleeve to take him inside, he fell straight forward. When she touched his head it was as cold as a rock, scaring her out of her wits.

"I was sitting right next to him when he breathed his last. I couldn't even raise his head. I couldn't do a thing," sobbed Ludrön.

"Don't cry, don't cry, recite *manis*, recite *manis*," said Sangyé, trying to stop her tears.

"I couldn't even get a cup of milk tea for him before he died. Not even a bite of *tsampa* with fresh butter. This morning he didn't eat anything but a bit of plain black *tsampa*. My poor dad . . ." Ludrön wept even more bitterly than before. Unable to bear it, Sangyé began to cry too. It really was awful that he couldn't manage to get his father-in-law a cup of tea or a bit of fresh butter before he passed, he thought. He felt ashamed at what a useless son-in-law he was. But it was no use having regrets. The best thing he could do for him now was to prepare the proper funeral rituals. Leaving Ludrön to mourn, he removed the inlaid saddle from the old piece of cloth in which it had been wrapped, hoisted it onto his shoulder, and prepared to head into town. But now he felt that he couldn't just leave the two women alone with the body, so he set the saddle down on the ground. He went outside, and just as he did the couple from the family next door, having heard the cries, came to see what was going on.

"My father-in-law passed away, all of a sudden," Sangyé told the husband. "Please, could I trouble you to stay with my wife and her mother for a bit while I go to town? I need to tell my family the news and see if I can find Alak Drong." Picking up the saddle again, he turned to leave, but stopped in his tracks and came back as though he had just realized something. Slowly raising the coat covering the body, he saw the old man still clutching his prayer beads in his left hand and a prayer wheel in his right. He was about to remove them when his older neighbor stopped him. "*Ah tsi ah tsi!*" he exclaimed. "This is a pious man. I think it's best if you leave them alone. If you want them removed, better to have a lama do it." So Sangyé covered him with the coat once more.

"We by you're used gods—best offer garanteed!" A sign in Tibetan filled with spelling mistakes hung outside the pawn shop, the letters resembling ant tracks in the dirt. After the owner had carefully examined each of the items brought by Sangyé—the saddle, stirrups, and other accessories—he raised a single finger, offering one *wan*—ten thousand yuan. Sangyé, misunderstanding, shook his head. "Well, how much money you want for it?" asked the owner in his crude Tibetan.

"Eight thousand."

"Eight thousand?"

"Eight thousand."

"Eight thousand. Eight thousand." The owner shook his head, not knowing whether to laugh or cry, and counted out the money.

Just as Sangyé left the pawn shop feeling quite pleased with himself, he saw Alak Drong getting out of a car. Rushing over, he told the lama that his father-in-law had suddenly passed away and beseeched him to pay a visit to his bedside. Much to his surprise, Alak Drong jumped back in the car, saying, "Come on then, let's go!" This put Sangyé in a fluster. "Of course . . . but . . . we haven't prepared anything . . . perhaps tomorrow . . ." Alak Drong barked his response as though he were issuing orders. "I'm going to Xining tomorrow. If you haven't got a vehicle, then jump in my *qiche*!"

Fortunately, Sangyé got home to find that some of the former inhabitants of Tsezhung County who now lived in Happy Ecological Resettlement Village had been phoning around and were already gathered at his house. Without much trouble at all they helped Sangyé arrange a date for the funeral and other matters with Alak Drong.

Alak Drong said a few words to guide the consciousness of the deceased to its appropriate destination and prepared to leave. "Venerable Rinpoché, please look at this," said one of the elderly neighbors, lifting up the fur coat to show him the beads and the prayer wheel clutched in the old man's hands. Unfortunately, apart from asking why on earth they hadn't removed those things from his hands, Alak Drong offered no other auspicious remarks.

ELEVEN

After the death of her husband, Yangdzom didn't get out of bed until late in the day. She no longer watched TV like she used to. Instead, she would go outside and sit where her husband used to sit on the doorstep, and there she would stay, staring toward the main gate, just waiting for Lhari Kyi to come home from school. When Lhari Kyi did get home, she always had even more news to report than the TV. Sadly, it was always about utterly horrifying events. For instance, she had had two pieces of news the day before. The first was that a number of students who boarded at the school had gotten food poisoning. Although they were sent to the hospital, five of them were beyond help and died. The second was that one of those many coal trucks, which were as big as mountains and flowed like rivers, had hit a small car containing four people and squashed it as flat as a steel plate.

Every time Yangdzom heard one of these stories she would close her eyes, clasp her hands to her chest, and offer a prayer: "By the Three Jewels, may all sentient beings be spared disasters like this." But how could she know that just such a disaster was about to befall her own family? It was a freezing cold, frosty morning. Lhari Kyi had left for school earlier than usual and Yangdzom was still in bed. Sangyé and Ludrön were outside, ripping up an old sash into strips of cloth and stuffing them into the cracks in the walls. Sangyé's mind wasn't on the work in front of him; it was on the news he'd heard that a place in town was looking to hire a security guard. At some point they both felt an unsteadiness in their legs, and in that instant, the entire row of houses collapsed before their very eyes, sending a cloud of black dust into the air that blocked out everything. They stood rooted to the spot, completely stunned. Somewhere nearby a man ran past, yelling, "Earthquake! Earthquake!" The two of them finally came to their senses and, almost in unison, called out "Mother!" They clawed desperately at the tiles and bricks as if they'd lost their minds. When they lifted off some beams that had collapsed over the folded-up tent, Sangyé and Ludrön were overjoyed to find Yangdzom lying in the space underneath, not so much as a scratch on her. Barely able to believe their eyes, they helped her up, asking repeatedly if she was hurt. When they were finally convinced that it was real, they thanked the compassion of the Three Jewels over and over again. Just then they saw a man running past, wailing at the top of his voice. "*Ah ho! Ah ho!* The students have all been crushed to a pulp!" Once again, almost in unison, they called out "Lhari Kyi!," jumped to their feet, and started to run.

To Yangdzom it seemed like a year, but in reality it was just an hour later that Sangyé returned, staggering as he held the lifeless, blood-soaked little body of Lhari Kyi. "Heaven is blind, heaven is blind . . ." he kept on moaning. Strangely, Ludrön didn't weep as she had when her father died; she simply shed a few silent tears and sighed.

As they later learned, this was only a magnitude 4.0 earthquake. Except for the Ecological Resettlement Villages and a few schools, it hadn't caused much damage. The government speedily arranged relief aid for those affected by the disaster in the form of emergency tents and food supplies. Not only did they provide compensation payments for the injured and the families of the dead, they promised that new houses would be built as soon as possible, even better and sturdier than the previous ones, and free of charge. The nomads were once again moved to tears of gratitude. But Sangyé's family had long since lost the desire to live there. They had only continued to put up with it for the sake of Lhari Kyi's schooling, but now that she was gone, there was no longer anything to keep them. And so, one morning, they hired a hand tractor and set off for Black Fox Valley.

The road home was clogged with those coal trucks that were as big as mountains and flowed like rivers, stirring up huge clouds of dust as they rushed back and forth, almost trampling—or rather flattening—the little tractor as they went. Ludrön, feeling even more dejected than before, rubbed her chest and sighed. It seemed that Sangyé too was feeling dejected. For the whole journey he plucked his moustache, not saying a word.

Since there were so many trucks, the tractor had to drive extremely slowly, and since they were driving so slowly, it wasn't until almost sunset that they finally arrived at the mountain pass of Black Fox Valley. Then they were confronted with a sight even more shocking and incomprehensible than that of Lhari Kyi's crushed little body. The entirety of Black Fox Valley had been dug up and turned into an expanse of pitch black. Everywhere you looked there were diggers, loaders, dump trucks, and tractors scurrying like ants from a nest, a seething maelstrom of activity. The roar of the machines sounded like a thousand thunderclaps booming at once.

So many new paths leading from the pass into the valley had appeared that the driver didn't know which one to take, so he hit the brakes and waited for instructions from his passenger. But not only did his passenger fail to utter a sound, he even forgot to pluck his moustache. After a moment he regained his senses and began to look around, thinking they must have taken a wrong turn. But apart from the fact that the cairn and the prayer flags had turned black, everything was the same, confirming that no, they had not.

"Now I understand why the foxes in this valley are black," Sangyé said.

Ludrön, who'd been silent the whole day, finally spoke. "So this is where all that expensive black rock comes from."

15

NOTES OF A VOLUNTEER AIDS WORKER

Shoot, you don't need to ask me(1) anything. I'll tell you everything. Tell it straight. Every last detail. You can record what I say, then you can write it up and print the whole thing. You can even put my real name and where I used to work. I've ruined everything anyway, so I don't need to worry about it anymore. My only hope is that people won't follow in my footsteps.

I am the former head of the Economics and Trade Department of XX(2) Prefecture, XX Province. My name is XX. I've taken some "bosses"(3) to the whorehouse a few times, but I always used a condom, so there's no way I got this damn disease from that. Shoot, so when did I get it? It was probably in 200X. Yeah, that it's for sure—the National Day in October that year. Boss Zhang from Sichuan gave me a bribe of two hundred thousand yuan, and I gave him the project worth four million. He couldn't have been happier, and he took me to the best restaurant in XX City. When we were playing mahjong he lost on purpose and gave me another 30,000-ish. After we'd had our fill of all the finest food and booze, he took me to a bathhouse. It was one of those places that's called a bathhouse, but you don't really go there for a wash, you go there for a prostitute. Shoot, there was this girl there—I picked her out from a lineup of three or four—she looked even younger than my youngest daughter. She was a sweet, beautiful thing, and best of all she had big, firm tits and a soft, round ass. From the look of her body, she seemed perfectly healthy. She said she was from up in the northeast, and judging from her fluent Mandarin, it seemed true. Either way, she was different from any girl, or prostitute, I'd met before. But I really don't want to talk about that girl now. She took a shower, then she said, "Brother, you're a handsome man, and you're healthy looking too, so you don't have to use a condom."

That made me hesitate for a moment. "That guy you came in with said I had to do everything I could to satisfy you and make you happy," she said with a grin; then she glued her lips to my crotch like a hungry baby presented with its mother's breast and I completely forgot about the condom—and everything else. Shoot, who knew that one moment of pleasure would destroy my whole life, and even destroy my whole family line? So yes, it was that woman who infected me with this damn disease for sure.

About six or seven years later I got a fever and my joints started to ache. At first I thought it was just an ordinary flu and didn't pay it much mind. But it got worse by the day, and the medicine and injections didn't help in the least. Then I started to lose weight, and sores appeared all over my body. The doctors in that small town ran test after test but still couldn't figure out what was wrong with me, so I had to go to the big hospital in the city. Shoot, it was there I finally discovered that "AIDS," this damn disease that I'd barely heard of before, that I thought was vastly removed from me, that didn't even have any connection to me at all, had, in fact, become a part of my body, and what's more was in the process of killing me. For a while I didn't believe it, and I went to an infectious diseases clinic to get a second opinion. Unfortunately, the results of their tests were exactly the same. Everything before my eyes turned dark gray and pitch black. . . .

It was then that I thought back and it finally occurred to me it was that bastard Boss Zhang who had thrown me into this fiery pit. And I finally realized that, even more than him, it was that goddamn prostitute who had thrown me into this hell. I was consumed by an overwhelming hatred of Boss Zhang. I was consumed by an overwhelming hatred of that prostitute. Even more than them, I was consumed by an overwhelming hatred of myself. But it's true what they say, "There's nothing worse than regret." I used to think that if you had status you had money, and if you had money then you had everything. I did whatever I could to take from my subordinates and give to my superiors and to strive to keep rising through the ranks. But I was completely wrong. Now I know that even if I were the dictator of my own country and had a mountain of gold at my disposal, it wouldn't be the slightest bit of use.

Shoot, then my throat and genitals started to . . . well, I don't need to tell you this, you're an AIDS worker, you get the idea. Anyway, my body started showing all these unimaginable symptoms, and I felt pain like I can't even describe. There was no cure anyway, so I thought about suicide, but it became clear to me that I had neither the means nor the will to kill myself. I finally realized that the family around me, even complete strangers, in fact everything in the whole world—the mountains and rivers, the plants, the houses and highways—it was all so beautiful and dear to me. But my physical and mental suffering still made me want to end it all, the sooner the better. I'm terrified of dying, but I'm even more terrified of living. I'm forever tormented by terrible hallucinations and nightmares. Sometimes I'm being hunted down by a bunch of cops with all these cutting-edge weapons, like the kind you see in the movies. Sometimes I get caught by gangsters; they hammer nails into my body and they cut my dick off, then they take off all my clothes and throw me into a huge square full of people. Sometimes my relatives, colleagues, doctors—even volunteers like you—grow five-foot tongues and ten-inch fangs, then peel off my skin, suck my blood, eat my flesh, and chew on my bones. Or they cut up my arms and legs and all my internal organs cell by cell, then use all these machines to do experiments and tests on them. Sometimes I'm in a deserted wilderness being chased by wild beasts, and they chase me and chase me until I fall into a bottomless abyss. I grab on to the branch of a tree but don't have the strength to pull myself up, so I have to just hang there in midair. Sometimes a bunch of girls, their bodies oozing pus and blood all over, strip me naked; then, moaning, they kiss me everywhere and suck my dick. . . .

Shoot, so now, as you can see, I'm living through hell on earth, neither a man nor a demon. What's worse is, even if I die, the thing I really can't take is that my wife too . . . if the next lives really do exist, then may I be born in all of them as sheep, yaks, and pigs under her butcher's knife! And my two daughters—they can't even show their faces in public, let alone find a man and get married. Now my family line is finished. I've become the enemy—the murderer, even—of my own family line. . . . I've made up my mind to do everything I can not to think about all this anymore. As it happens, the pain doesn't give you the chance to do much thinking anyway. But sometimes I can't help but be reminded of it all, and it torments me even more than before.

Shoot, it wasn't until later, when I met AIDS volunteers like yourself, that I found out Tibet is full of AIDS victims just like me, and what's more the number is getting bigger and bigger. So that's why I've told you everything and held absolutely nothing back. My goal is for people not to follow in my footsteps. I hope that you'll put out what I've said here just like I told it to you. Shoot, sorry, I'm really tired now. I don't even have the energy to speak. Sorry . . .

Notes

1. The patient referred to here as "I" died suddenly two weeks to the day after I interviewed him. A year after that his wife also died.
2. I have substituted "XX" for place names, personal names, etc.
3. I have here translated into Tibetan the many Chinese words, such as *gongtou* (boss), that my interview subject made liberal use of in his speech.

WEATHERHEAD BOOKS ON ASIA

WEATHERHEAD EAST ASIAN INSTITUTE,
COLUMBIA UNIVERSITY

LITERATURE

DAVID DER-WEI WANG, EDITOR

Kim Sowŏl, *Azaleas: A Book of Poems*, translated by David McCann
(2007)

Wang Anyi, *The Song of Everlasting Sorrow: A Novel of Shanghai*,
translated by Michael Berry with Susan Chan Egan (2008)

Ch'oe Yun, *There a Petal Silently Falls: Three Stories by Ch'oe Yun*, translated by Bruce and Ju-Chan Fulton (2008)

Inoue Yasushi, *The Blue Wolf: A Novel of the Life of Chinggis Khan*,
translated by Joshua A. Fogel (2009)

Anonymous, *Courtesans and Opium: Romantic Illusions of the Fool of
Yangzhou*, translated by Patrick Hanan (2009)

Cao Naiqian, *There's Nothing I Can Do When I Think of You Late at
Night*, translated by John Balcom (2009)

Park Wan-suh, *Who Ate Up All the Shinga? An Autobiographical Novel*,
translated by Yu Young-nan and Stephen J. Epstein (2009)

Yi T'aejun, *Eastern Sentiments*, translated by Janet Poole (2009)

Hwang Sunwŏn, *Lost Souls: Stories*, translated by Bruce and Ju-Chan
Fulton (2009)

Kim Sŏk-pŏm, *The Curious Tale of Mandogi's Ghost*, translated by
Cindi Textor (2010)

The Columbia Anthology of Modern Chinese Drama, edited by Xiaomei
Chen (2011)

Qian Zhongshu, *Humans, Beasts, and Ghosts: Stories and Essays*, edited
by Christopher G. Rea, translated by Dennis T. Hu, Nathan K.
Mao, Yiran Mao, Christopher G. Rea, and Philip F. Williams
(2011)

Dung Kai-cheung, *Atlas: The Archaeology of an Imaginary City*, translated by Dung Kai-cheung, Anders Hansson, and Bonnie S.
McDougall (2012)

O Chŏnghŭi, *River of Fire and Other Stories*, translated by Bruce and Ju-Chan Fulton (2012)

Endō Shūsaku, *Kiku's Prayer: A Novel*, translated by Van Gessel (2013)

Li Rui, *Trees Without Wind: A Novel*, translated by John Balcom (2013)

Abe Kōbō, *The Frontier Within: Essays by Abe Kōbō*, edited, translated, and with an introduction by Richard F. Calichman (2013)

Zhu Wen, *The Matchmaker, the Apprentice, and the Football Fan: More Stories of China*, translated by Julia Lovell (2013)

The Columbia Anthology of Modern Chinese Drama, Abridged Edition, edited by Xiaomei Chen (2013)

Natsume Sōseki, *Light and Dark*, translated by John Nathan (2013)

Seirai Yūichi, *Ground Zero, Nagasaki: Stories*, translated by Paul Warham (2015)

Hideo Furukawa, *Horses, Horses, in the End the Light Remains Pure: A Tale That Begins with Fukushima*, translated by Doug Slaymaker with Akiko Takenaka (2016)

Abe Kōbō, *Beasts Head for Home: A Novel*, translated by Richard F. Calichman (2017)

Yi Mun-yol, *Meeting with My Brother: A Novella*, translated by Heinz Insu Fenkl with Yoosup Chang (2017)

Ch'ae Manshik, *Sunset: A Ch'ae Manshik Reader*, edited and translated by Bruce and Ju-Chan Fulton (2017)

Tanizaki Jun'ichiro, *In Black and White: A Novel*, translated by Phyllis I. Lyons (2018)

Yi T'aejun, *Dust and Other Stories*, translated by Janet Poole (2018)

HISTORY, SOCIETY, AND CULTURE

CAROL GLUCK, EDITOR

Takeuchi Yoshimi, *What Is Modernity? Writings of Takeuchi Yoshimi*, edited and translated, with an introduction, by Richard F. Calichman (2005)

Contemporary Japanese Thought, edited and translated by Richard F. Calichman (2005)

Overcoming Modernity, edited and translated by Richard F. Calichman (2008)

Natsume Sōseki, *Theory of Literature and Other Critical Writings*, edited and translated by Michael Bourdaghs, Atsuko Ueda, and Joseph A. Murphy (2009)

Kojin Karatani, *History and Repetition*, edited by Seiji M. Lippit (2012)

The Birth of Chinese Feminism: Essential Texts in Transnational Theory, edited by Lydia H. Liu, Rebecca E. Karl, and Dorothy Ko (2013)

Yoshiaki Yoshimi, *Grassroots Fascism: The War Experience of the Japanese People*, translated by Ethan Mark (2015)